"I thought we'd have ~~some~~ ~~something about~~
our new relationship ~~she told her in~~
his best Southern-gentleman drawl.

"Our relationship?" Alisha echoed incredulously.

"Landlord and tenant," Brett replied, indicating first himself, then her. "Why? What did you think I was referring to?"

Still sitting on the stool, she squared her shoulders. "I didn't have a clue," she lied. "That's why I asked."

"You want something light and fruity—or something hard?" he asked her.

The words seemed disconnected as they came out of the blue like that. Confused, she could only ask, "What?" as she stared at him.

"To drink," Brett prompted. "Light and fruity—" he gestured toward the small array of bottles filled with colorful mixed drinks "—or hard?" he concluded, waving a hand toward the bottles that contained alcohol his customers downed straight.

"What did you just have?" she asked, nodding at his empty shot glass.

"Wild Turkey, 101 proof," he told her.

She pushed her glass to one side and said, "I'll have the same."

Brett looked at her uncertainly. "Are you sure?" he asked. "It's rather strong and you might get more than you bargained for."

Her eyes locked with Brett's. "I think I already have."

Dear Reader,

Welcome back to Forever, Texas. Last time around, we saw the last of the Rodriguez brothers find the woman of his dreams right under his nose. In this book, I'm ushering in a new family, three brothers who found themselves orphaned at an early age and were taken in by their uncle Patrick, their late father's older brother. Patrick was entrusted with running Murphy's, the generations-old family-owned saloon (more than just a bar, a place where men and women feel comfortable going just to talk and grab a social drink—or soda). When Patrick suddenly became ill and died, the establishment was passed on to the three brothers: Brett, Finn and Liam. Since Brett Murphy was the only one who was of age, running the place—and keeping his small family intact—fell to him. Brett is the backbone of this family, having given up a great deal to make sure that his brothers are safe, together and properly educated. While he's a charmer, there was only one woman he ever loved, and she made him choose between her and his family. He chose his family.

Dr. Alisha Cordell had her life all mapped out. A resident at a top New York teaching hospital, she was engaged to a neurosurgeon from a fine old family. The problem was that while his family was fine, he was not and a breakup between the two was inevitable. Nursing her broken heart, Alisha sees a letter on the hospital bulletin board from a Dr. Dan Davenport looking for a physician willing to come to Forever and work at his clinic. It seems like fate—but is it? Come read and find out.

As always, I thank you for reading my latest offering. I hope it entertains you. And from the bottom of my heart, I wish you someone to love who loves you back.

All the best,

Marie

HER FOREVER COWBOY

MARIE FERRARELLA

HARLEQUIN® AMERICAN ROMANCE®

Recycling programs for this product may not exist in your area.

ISBN-13: 978-0-373-75534-9

HER FOREVER COWBOY

Copyright © 2014 by Marie Rydzynski-Ferrarella

All rights reserved. Except for use in any review, the reproduction or utilization of this work in whole or in part in any form by any electronic, mechanical or other means, now known or hereinafter invented, including xerography, photocopying and recording, or in any information storage or retrieval system, is forbidden without the written permission of the publisher, Harlequin Enterprises Limited, 225 Duncan Mill Road, Don Mills, Ontario M3B 3K9, Canada.

This is a work of fiction. Names, characters, places and incidents are either the product of the author's imagination or are used fictitiously, and any resemblance to actual persons, living or dead, business establishments, events or locales is entirely coincidental.

This edition published by arrangement with Harlequin Books S.A.

For questions and comments about the quality of this book, please contact us at CustomerService@Harlequin.com.

® and TM are trademarks of Harlequin Enterprises Limited or its corporate affiliates. Trademarks indicated with ® are registered in the United States Patent and Trademark Office, the Canadian Intellectual Property Office and in other countries.

Printed in U.S.A.

ABOUT THE AUTHOR

This *USA TODAY* bestselling and RITA® Award-winning author has written more than two hundred books for Harlequin, some under the name Marie Nicole. Her romances are beloved by fans worldwide. Visit her website, www.marieferrarella.com.

Books by Marie Ferrarella

To
Pat Teal,
who, 33 years ago,
said to me,
"Have you thought about writing a romance?"
Rest in peace, Pat.
I miss you.

Prologue

No one looking at her would have suspected that her heart had just been broken, or even bruised. She made sure of that.

Dr. Alisha Cordell prided herself on being self-contained. She wasn't the type to let people in on her private hurt. Nor would she allow herself to shed tears. At least, not publicly.

Publicly, if she included the half-naked hospital administrator closeted with her fiancé as being part of the general public, the only display of emotion anyone had witnessed was when she'd thrown her three-carat diamond engagement ring at Dr. Pierce Belkin—a neurosurgeon who was much in demand, not always by his patients—and the aforementioned hospital administrator.

A flash of fury had accompanied the flying ring as well as a single seething word that wasn't part of her usual vocabulary.

It hadn't even been the sight of the ruggedly handsome *Mayflower* descendant making love to the vapid, overly endowed blonde that had made Alisha throw her ring at him. It was Pierce's complete lack of contrition coupled with the snide remark—"Oh, grow up, Alisha.

Just because we're getting married doesn't mean I'm going to be your slave"—that made her lose her composure and had her throwing the ring and then telling Pierce to take up residence in a much hotter location.

The story was *already* making the rounds by the time she'd taken the elevator from the fifth floor down to the first. Not that she cared about the gossip. She'd never been the kind to pay any attention to whispers. But what convinced Alisha that she needed a change of scenery was the fact that although the hospital was far from a small place, there was no doubt in her mind that she wouldn't be able to avoid running into Pierce *or* any of what she had come to realize were his numerous conquests.

Good at shutting out things that irritated her, Alisha still knew that she would be able to hold her head high for only so long before the situation would become intolerable to her.

There was no way around it. She needed to find somewhere else to be. Preferably somewhere far away.

As a rule, Alisha didn't make friends easily. Dedicated, driven, she'd ignored socializing to focus on becoming the best all-around general surgeon she could be. In part—a large part—to honor her father.

A giant of a man, Dr. William Cordell had been a family-practice physician. Alisha was his only child, and she had adored him. A nature enthusiast, he would go camping whenever he could get away. His wife hadn't shared his interest in the great outdoors, but Alisha had, and he had taken her with him, teaching her all the fundamentals of survival.

Cancer had abruptly ended her father's life when she was just fourteen. She'd never been close to her mother, and the two had drifted even further apart after that. Alisha closed herself off emotionally and worked on achieving her goal to the exclusion of almost everything else. It kept her father's memory alive for her.

The people she'd been thrown in with at college studied hard but partied harder. She remained on the outside fringes of that world. Looking back, she realized that the only reason Pierce had pursued her with such vigor was because she was the only female who had ever said no to him. He viewed her as a challenge as well as a budding gifted surgeon. In time, he thought of her as a worthy extension of himself, a professional asset.

Added to that, his parents liked her, and his grandmother, a very wealthy woman, was crazy about her. She'd referred to her as her grandson's *saving grace* and wholeheartedly looked forward to their wedding.

Secretly missing the comforting security of a home life, Alisha had accepted Pierce's proposal despite the uneasiness she experienced when she'd actually uttered the word *yes*. Her uneasiness refused to completely go away even as the weeks went by.

She should have gone with her gut. Alisha upbraided herself after the engagement ring—a family heirloom—had left her finger. It was her gut that had told her to turn Pierce down; her gut that told her that a so-called fairy-tale wedding and marriage were *not* in the cards for her, not with this self-centered Adonis. But loneliness was a powerful persuader, and she really had liked his family. In a moment of weakness, she'd agreed.

And now she was paying for it, Alisha thought ruefully.

The worst part was that this was *not* the first time she'd caught Pierce being unfaithful. But in each case, it had been after the fact, certainly not *during* the act, the way it had been this last time. And those other times, he'd made apologetic noises that she'd accepted. This time, there hadn't even been the pretense of regret or remorse. If there *was* any regret about the incident, it was that he had gotten caught, nothing beyond that.

Well, her engagement—and Pierce—were now part of her past, and she wanted no reminders, no chance encounters to haunt her and make her uncomfortable, even inwardly. It didn't matter how good a poker face she could maintain, she didn't want to be reminded of her near-terminal mistake.

Moving away was not a problem. But finding a destination was. Where could she go? As if some unseen force was taking matters in hand, Alisha became aware of the fact that she was pondering her fate standing next to the physicians' bulletin board, the one where almost anything could be found by those who had the patience to carefully scan the different missives tacked onto that board. There were courtside tickets to the next basketball game being offered for sale—or more accurately, resale—slightly used furniture *in reasonable shape* could be gotten for a song and so on. All in all, it was like a visual bazaar without the noise.

For a fleeting moment, looking at the bulletin board, it occurred to Alisha that she could have offered her engagement ring up for sale, but she decided that throwing it at Pierce was infinitely more satisfying than any money she could have gotten for it.

Besides, it had belonged to his grandmother, and she had liked the woman.

That was when she spotted it. A letter tacked on the upper left corner of the bulletin board. It was almost obscured by an ad for a *European cruise of a lifetime*. Moving the ad aside, she saw that the neatly typed letter was addressed to "Any budding, selfless physician reading this letter who might be willing to put in long hours for very little financial reward, reaping instead endless emotional satisfaction that he or she was making a difference in some good people's lives." There was more written after that, an entire long paragraph, describing the conditions in the area as well as summarizing the basic requirements. It was signed by a Dr. Daniel Davenport.

Alisha stared at the letter for a minute or so before she finally took it down to read more carefully.

Was this Dr. Daniel Davenport for real, sending something like this here? Alisha wondered. The recently graduated physicians at this teaching hospital were all aiming at practices that would have them working a minimum of hours for a maximum financial return. This letter sounded as if it was an appeal for a saint, or at the very least, for a doctor who was willing to travel to a third-world country on a regular basis.

Well, you wanted to get away. This certainly qualifies as getting away, a voice in her head pointed out.

Alisha stared at the address at the top of the letter. This Dr. Davenport lived somewhere called "Forever, Texas."

Alisha frowned. Okay, not a third-world country, but she still hadn't heard of the place. But then, she hadn't heard of a great many places, and this Forever certainly sounded as if it was far away enough to qualify as *getting away*.

Alisha stared at the letter, weighing her options. The

one thing she knew was that she did *not* want to remain
here a second longer than she had to.

After a moment's internal debate, rather than tack the
letter back up on the bulletin board, she carefully folded
it and put the letter in the pocket of her white lab coat.

Forever, Alisha mused. It had an interesting ring to it.

Chapter One

"Pinch me, brother."

Brett Murphy, one-third owner of Murphy's and the older brother of the other two-thirds owners, Finn and Liam, paused wiping down the long, sleek counter of Forever's only saloon as he saw Dr. Dan Davenport, walking by the establishment's tinted bay window.

It was not the town's only physician who had caught Brett's attention but the tall, willowy young woman who was walking beside Dan. The tall, willowy young woman who was *not* Dan's wife, Tina, or Holly Rodriguez, his new nurse.

"Why?" Liam asked, only half listening to him.

Though the saloon wasn't actually open yet, and certainly not ready to go into full swing for a number of hours, Liam was doing a preliminary instrument check—for the second time. He and his budding band were playing here tonight, and Brett had raised him never to leave anything to chance or take anything for granted. Liam had his eye on someday leaving the saloon behind him and going professional.

Though he was seldom mesmerized by *anything,* Dan's companion had managed to completely captivate him, even at this distance.

Now, that is one gorgeous woman, Brett couldn't help thinking.

"Because, little brother," he said aloud, "I think I've just seen the woman of my dreams."

That managed to get Liam's attention. His guitar temporarily forgotten, Liam looked up at his oldest brother then turned to see what Brett was talking about.

At that point, the young woman who had so completely caught Brett's fancy had disappeared from view. Her presence was replaced by another female who was passing by. Mildred Haggerty.

Liam's jaw slackened and dropped as he turned back to look at his brother.

"Mrs. Haggerty is the woman of your dreams?" he asked incredulously. "Have you had your eyes checked lately? Better yet, have you had your *head* checked lately?" Liam asked.

Mildred Haggerty was as tall as she was wide, had an overbearing personality with an unabashed drive to dominate everyone she came in contact with. A woman of some independent means, in her lifetime, she had buried three husbands. Rumor had it that they had all died willingly in order to permanently get away from the source of their misery, Mildred.

Brett looked at Liam as if the latter was the one who had lost his mind. But before Brett could remark on it, the front door began to creak, announcing that someone was disregarding the hours that were posted outside and coming into Murphy's. In general, Brett was rather flexible about adhering to the hours carved into the sign, enforcing them when the whim hit him. He was not above welcoming the lone, stray customer before hours.

Thinking that Mrs. Haggerty was the one entering—

possibly trolling for husband number four—Liam took it upon himself to loudly announce, "We're not really open for business yet."

"How about pleasure?" Dr. Dan Davenport asked as he held the door open for the reason he had come to Murphy's in the first place. The young woman accompanying him walked into the saloon, squinting slightly as her eyes became accustomed to the darkened interior. "Are you open for pleasure?" Dan asked, a broad grin on his lips.

All in all, the physician looked like a man who had just caught hold of a lifeline, one he hadn't really expected to materialize, Brett thought.

His green eyes slowly traveled over the length of the woman who'd been ushered in by the town's only doctor. Brett took in her long, straight blond hair, her fair complexion and her almost hypnotically blue eyes.

If possible, the woman looked even better close-up than she did at a distance.

"Pleasure it is," Brett acknowledged, wondering who this woman was and, more important, if she was staying in town for an extended visit. Was she a friend of the doctor's, or perhaps a friend of Dan's wife, Tina, neither of whom were actual natives of the town?

Dan inclined his head, picking up Brett's answer. "Then it's my sincere pleasure to introduce you two to the lady who answered my ad—and my prayers." For his part, Dan resembled a little boy who had woken up on Christmas morning to discover that everything he had asked for was right there, beneath the Christmas tree.

"You advertised for an angel?" Brett asked, putting his own interpretation to Dan's introduction.

Alisha Cordell had always had sharp eyes that missed very little. She narrowed them now as she looked at the man behind the bar.

This dark-haired, green-eyed bartender fancied himself a charmer, a smooth talker, she thought with an accompanying degree of contempt. The contempt rose to the surface as a matter of course. After Pierce, she'd had more than her fill of good-looking men who felt they were God's gift to women. Her conclusion had been that the better-looking they were, the worse they were.

"Dr. Davenport advertised for a doctor," she informed the would-be Romeo massaging the counter in no uncertain terms.

The look she gave the man just stopped short of being contemptuous. If this two-bit cowboy thought she would instantly become smitten with him because he was clearly handsome and capable of spouting trite compliments, he was going to be very sorely disappointed, Alisha silently predicted. She hoped the rest of the men in town weren't like this.

And if she was going to be staying in this dusty little burg, even for a little while, this cowboy—and anyone else who might share the same stereotypical mind-set—needed to be put in his—and their—place, as well as on notice that she wasn't here to indulge their fantasies. The only reason she was here and would even entertain the idea of remaining here was to help Dr. Davenport heal their wounds and take care of their ills.

Nothing else.

Brett detected the flicker of fire in her eyes, and his grin widened. "Well, I think I'm getting feverish, so I just might wind up being your very first patient," he told what was hopefully Forever's newest resident.

Alisha took a certain amount of pleasure shooting the sexy bartender down.

"I'm just here to observe for the first few days, so I'm afraid that Dr. Davenport would be the one who'll have to treat your fever," she informed him crisply.

Dan cleared his throat and launched into introductions. "Brett and Liam Murphy," he said, waving a hand at first one, then the other of the brothers as he said their names for Alisha's benefit, "I'd like you both to meet Dr. Alisha Cordell. Dr. Cordell," he went on, reciprocating the introduction, "Brett and Liam. They're two-thirds of the owners of Murphy's, Forever's only saloon."

Brett inclined his head. "Pleased to have you in Forever," he told her. His voice became only a tad more serious as he said to her, "The doc here could really use the help."

"I'm sure," Alisha replied, sounding exceedingly formal.

She hadn't wanted to be impolite to the doctor, but she'd tried to tell him that this tour of the town and its residents was really unnecessary. She'd come here to practice medicine, to answer the call for a physician, not concern herself with socializing. After the fiasco with Pierce, she'd had more than enough of *socializing* to last her for a very long time.

Possibly forever. The irony of that thought was not lost on her.

But since she was here, Alisha thought with resignation, she might as well pretend she was taking the scenery—and its people—in.

Alisha scanned the saloon slowly. The place had an exceedingly rustic look to it, as if the building had been here for at least the past seven or eight decades, if not longer.

Was this the extent of the diversion that the town had to offer? she wondered in disbelief.

"And this is where people come for a *night out?*" she asked, not bothering to hide the incredulous note in her voice.

"Dr. Cordell is from New York," Dan felt obligated to tell the two men. It wasn't an apology so much as an explanation for the obvious disbelief in the young woman's voice.

He'd come from New York himself, although at this point, it felt as if that had been a hundred years ago instead of just four. At the time, it hadn't even been a sense of altruism that had brought him here. Guilt had been the emotion that was responsible for bringing him to Forever.

Guilt and a sense of obligation.

He felt he owed it to Warren. Warren had been his younger brother, and a more quietly dedicated human being hadn't ever walked the face of the earth. He'd been the one to fatefully convince Warren to come out on one last night on the town before Warren left for the godforsaken dot on the map where he intended to set up a practice. Forever hadn't had a doctor for thirty years and was in desperate need of one within its borders.

A car accident that night had claimed Warren's life while leaving him with nothing more than an outward scratch. Internally, though, was another matter. For weeks afterward, he had been all but hemorrhaging guilt. But even so, he'd initially planned to stay in Forever only until a suitable replacement for his late brother could be located.

He hadn't counted on falling in love—with the town and with Tina Blayne, a single mother and the sheriff's sister-in-law.

Life truly happened while you were making other plans, Dan thought now. And while he didn't expect this young woman who had responded to his letter to feel the same way about the town, he had to admit that he was secretly hoping that she would in time.

"New York, eh? Don't worry," Brett assured Dan, even though his eyes never left the woman. "We won't hold that against her."

Alisha raised her chin, as if she had just been challenged. Of late, she knew she had gotten extremely touchy, but knowing didn't seem to help her rein in that feeling.

"Why should you?" she asked.

Brett didn't take offense at her tone. Rather, he just rolled with it, asking, "Short on senses of humor back in New York, are they?"

Alisha never missed a beat. "Not when something's funny," she said.

"Feisty," Brett pronounced, this time directing the comment toward the senior doctor. The grin on the bartender's face seemed to grow only sexier as he observed with approval. "She might just survive out here, then."

Dan made a quick judgment call, seeing the need to usher the young woman out before barbs began being exchanged. "Let me bring you over to Miss Joan's," Dan suggested.

Alisha glanced over at him, trying to hide her uneasiness. "That's not a brothel, is it?"

Brett was the first to succumb, laughing at the idea of the vivacious septuagenarian and diner owner who was part of all their lives for longer than anyone could remember running a house of ill repute. Liam quickly followed, and Dan held out for almost a minute, biting his tongue and trying to think of other things.

But the very image of the redheaded Miss Joan as a madam proved to be too much for him, as well, and he laughed until his sides ached, all the while trying to apologize to a less-than-entertained Alisha.

"I take it the answer's no," Alisha surmised, doing her best to maintain her dignity amid this joke she felt was at her expense.

It was Brett who answered her because Dan appeared to still be struggling for control. "Miss Joan runs the local diner. She dispenses hot food and sage advice, depending on what you need most. She's been here for as long as anyone can remember. Longer, probably. The diner's also the place where everyone goes to socialize when they're not—"

"Here, drinking," Alisha said, reaching the only conclusion that she could, given the facts as she perceived them.

Brett corrected her. "When they're not here socializing." His manner remained easygoing, but he wasn't about to allow misinformation to make the rounds. Murphy's wasn't only his livelihood, a way that had allowed him to raise his brothers while keeping an eye on them; it was also his heritage. The saloon had been passed on to him after his uncle had died. Before that, his late father had run the establishment. To Brett, Murphy's was almost as much of a living entity as his brothers were.

"Don't they come here to get drunk?" Alisha pressed, recalling some of the parties that had gone on after hours while she was attending medical school. Nobody drank for the taste or to just pass away an hour; they drank to get drunk and even more uninhibited than they already were.

Out of the corner of his eye, Brett saw that his brother was taking offense at the image the young doctor was painting. He wanted to set this woman straight before something regrettable might be said. Liam was soft-spoken and he meant well, but a lasting relationship between his brain and his tongue hadn't quite been reached yet.

"Not nearly as much as you would think," Brett told her, keeping his smile firmly in place. "I'm not sure exactly how it is in New York, but out here, we do look out for each other—and that includes knowing when to cut a customer off."

"Except for Nathan McLane," Liam interjected. The youngest Murphy brother was nothing if not painfully honest—to a fault, Brett sometimes thought.

Alisha looked from Liam to Dan. "Who's Nathan McLane?"

"A man who's married to the world's most overbearing wife," Brett answered. "Nathan has a very strong reason to come here and drown his sorrows."

"So you let him get drunk?" she asked, trying to get the story straight.

Brett caught the slight note of disapproval in her voice. "It's either that, or raise the bail for his release because the poor guy's going to strangle that woman someday just to get her to stop nagging him."

Alisha frowned. The dark-haired man was making it sound as if he was doing a good thing. "How noble of you."

Brett didn't rise to the bait. He was not about to argue

with the woman. He wasn't in the business of changing people's minds, only in telling it the way he saw it. "Dunno about *noble,* but it does keep everyone alive," he informed her.

Dan lightly took hold of Alisha's arm, wanting to usher her out while the young doctor who could very well be the answer to his prayers was still willing to remain in Forever and lend him a hand.

Glancing over her head, he indicated to Brett that he had a feeling that if his new *recruit* remained here, talking to him for a few more minutes, she might be on the first flight out of the nearby airport—headed back to New York.

"Next stop, Miss Joan's *Diner,*" Dan announced.

"Hey, Lady Doc," Brett called after her. Pausing by the door, she turned to spare him a glance. "Nice meeting you."

"Yes," she replied coolly. "You, too." The door closed behind them.

"Wow, if that was any colder, we'd have to bring out the pickaxes to break up the ice around you," Liam commented.

Brett saw no reason to dispute that assessment. However, true to his ever increasingly optimistic, positive nature, he pointed out, "That means that we can only go up from here."

Liam shook his head. It was clear that wasn't what he would have come away with. "You know, Brett, when I was a kid, I never thought of you as being the optimistic type."

"When you were a kid, you never thought," Brett reminded him with an infectious, deep laugh. Then he pretended to regard his brother for a moment before saying, "Come to think of it, you haven't really changed all that much—"

"Yeah, yeah," Liam said, shaking his head as he waved away his brother's comment. Glancing toward the door, he asked Brett, "Think she'll stay? She didn't look too impressed with the place."

"Neither was Dan when he first arrived," Brett reminded his brother. "But Forever's got a lot of positive things going for it, and besides, it's got a way of growing on people."

"Yeah," Liam laughed shortly as he went back to checking out the musical instruments. "Well, so does fungus."

"And that, little brother, is one of the reasons why no one's ever going to come up to you and ask you to write the travel brochure for Forever," Brett said wryly.

Liam looked at him quizzically. "Forever's got a travel brochure?"

Brett sighed and shook his head. "Sometimes, Liam, I do despair that all that higher education you were supposed to acquire while I was here, slaving away to pay the bills, was just leaking out your ear as fast as it went in."

Liam frowned at his brother, but his mood left as quickly as it had materialized. Ever since he was a child, it was a known fact that Liam didn't have it in him to stay mad at anyone, least of all his brothers.

Finished with what he was doing, Liam went on to step two of his process. "I've got to go round up the band and make sure everything's set for tonight."

Brett nodded as he went back to cleaning an already gleaming counter. He wasn't content until there were at least two coats of polish on it, buffed and dried.

"You do that, Liam," he told his brother. "You do that—just as long as you remember to get back here by six."

Liam stopped just short of opening the front door. "I don't go on until nine," he reminded Brett.

"Right," Brett agreed, sparing his brother a glance before getting back to polishing, "but you're tending bar at six. Tonight's our busy night," he added in case Liam had lost track of the days, "and I can't manage a full house alone."

"Get Finn," Liam told him. "He doesn't have anything else to do."

Brett caught his brother's meaning. That he felt he had found his calling and wanted to be free to put all his energy toward it.

"Don't belittle your brother just because he hasn't found his heart's passion yet," Brett chided. "It doesn't come to everyone at the same time."

"How about you, Brett? What's your passion?" Liam asked.

"I like running the bar." He made no apologies for it. His running the bar had been the family's saving grace. Rather than feel restrained by it, he was grateful for it and enjoyed being the one in charge of the place.

But Liam looked at him in disbelief. "And that's it? Nothing else?"

Brett took no offense at the incredulous tone. Liam was young and couldn't understand anyone who had a different focus, or aspirations that differed from his. He'd learn, Brett thought.

Out loud he said, "I like having my brothers pitch in without having to listen to some complicated internal argument that they feel obliged to repeat for me out loud."

Liam's handsome baby face scrunched up for a moment, as if thinking took every shred of concentration he had at his disposal. "That's supposed to put me in my place, isn't it?" he asked.

Brett flashed a tolerant grin at him. "Nice to know that all my money for your higher education *wasn't* completely misplaced. Okay, go," he said, waving Liam out the door. "Get your band ready and get back here by six."

The expression on Liam's face testified that he'd thought this argument had been resolved in his favor. "But—"

Brett pretended he didn't hear his brother's protest.

"With luck, I'll get Finn to help. He doesn't whine," he added for good measure.

"Oh, he whines. You just don't hear him" were Liam's parting words.

But Brett had already tuned him out. There were still things to see to before Murphy's officially opened its doors for the evening.

Chapter Two

"It's open, but I'm not serving yet," Brett called out in response to the light knock on the saloon's front door.

He thought it rather unusual that anyone would be knocking rather than just trying the doorknob and walking in. Most everyone in town knew that the door was unlocked not just during normal business hours—hours that extended way into the night—but also during non-business hours if any one of the Murphys were down on the ground floor. The only time the doors were locked was if they were all out or if one of them was upstairs.

The upper floor housed a small apartment that had once been occupied by Patrick Murphy, their father's older brother, when he was alive and running the family establishment. Although Brett and his brothers lived in a house close to Murphy's, there were times when Brett stayed in the apartment after putting in an exceptionally long night, too tired to walk home. And there were those times when he just wanted to grab a little time away from everyone in order to recharge batteries that were almost perpetually in use.

"That's fine because I'm not drinking yet," Olivia Santiago replied as she walked into Murphy's.

Turning around to look at the tall, slender blonde,

one of Forever's two lawyers, Brett was more than a little surprised to see the woman here at this hour—and
alone. It wasn't even noon.

He stopped restocking and came to the bar closest
to the front door. "And to what do I owe the pleasure
of having the sheriff's wife grace my establishment?"

"I'm not here as Rick's wife," Olivia told him, sliding onto a bar stool.

Brett reached for a bottle of ginger ale, knowing that
was the lawyer's beverage of choice before six o'clock.
Taking a glass, he filled it and then moved it in front
of her, before pouring one for himself.

He took into account the way she was dressed. Olivia
had on a dark gray jacket and a straight matching skirt.
A soft pink shirt added a touch of warmth to her appearance. Nonetheless, she was dressed for business.

"Then this is an official visit?" he surmised.

"If you mean am I here as a lawyer, the answer's
yes," she confirmed, then paused to take a sip.

"Someone suing us?" Brett asked, unable to think
of any other reason she'd be here in her professional
capacity. Even so, he couldn't think of a single reason
anyone would be suing them.

Olivia's mouth curved. "Should they be?" she asked
after taking another long sip from her glass.

Brett paused for a moment, as if giving her question due consideration. "Can't think of anyone who'd
want to, but both my only relatives are accounted for
and alive, so I can't think of another reason for you to
be here at this hour like this."

"Maybe I decided to take a break from work," she
suggested.

"You're a workaholic. You don't take a break. I don't

think you even stopped to take a breath after you gave birth." Births and deaths were very big events in a town the size of Forever. Each were duly noted and remembered by one and all.

"Oh, no, I stopped," Olivia assured him with feeling. "Trust me, having a child is a pretty life-altering event. You have to stop whatever else you're doing in order to absorb the full impact."

"I wouldn't know firsthand, but I'm not about to dispute that," he told her. He nodded at her glass and asked, "Can I get you anything else?"

Slight confusion creased her brow. "I thought that you and Miss Joan had an agreement. She doesn't serve any alcoholic beverages, and you don't serve any food."

"We do and I don't," he confirmed. "But I've got several kinds of nuts to offer my customers." Then, by way of an explanation in case, as a lawyer, she viewed that as a deal breaker, he said, "I don't think anyone really considers nuts to be food."

"Don't tell that to the squirrels," she commented, then smiled. "I'm fine," she assured him before adding, "No nuts. Thanks."

Brett shrugged as he returned to restocking the bar. "Don't mention it. Any time I can not get you something, just let me know."

Olivia remained silent for a few minutes, as if waiting. She smiled at Brett when he turned around again to pick up another bottle of alcohol.

"You're not going to ask, are you?" she marveled. "You have an amazing lack of curiosity. Either that, or you have remarkable restraint."

"It's not that," Brett replied. "If there's one thing I've learned on the other side of this bar, it's that if someone has something to say, you give them enough time, they'll tell you—if only to get it off their chest. All I have to do is wait—and if there's one thing I've gotten really good at, it's waiting."

Olivia bided her time until he'd set down the two bottles of vodka in his hands before telling him, "That's not the only thing you're good at, apparently."

"Okay, *now* I'm curious," Brett admitted. "That comment's going to need some explaining."

Olivia leaned slightly over the bar, her body language calling for his undivided attention even though they were the only two people in the bar. "Do you remember Earl Robertson?"

He thought for a moment—not because he couldn't put a face to the name, but because he was trying to remember the last time he'd seen the man who had been a friend of his father's. It had to have been at least three years since the man left town. Maybe more.

"Sure, I remember Earl. He took off to live in Taos, New Mexico. Said he always wanted to see that part of the country."

He didn't add that he had tried to persuade the man to stay. Earl had been getting on in years, and as far as he could tell, the man had no friends or family in Taos. No one to look out for him. But to suggest that would have meant wounding the man's pride, and that was something he hadn't been willing to do. For some men, pride was all they had. That was the case with Earl.

"What's he doing these days?" he asked, keeping his tone light.

"Not much of anything," Olivia replied. "Earl Robertson died last week."

The words hit harder than he'd expected. The man

wasn't family, but at this point, Earl was the closest thing to family he and his brothers still had. He felt he owed the old man a lot.

"Oh, I'm sorry to hear that. He was a good guy," Brett said after a beat.

"Apparently," Olivia went on, "Mr. Robertson thought the same thing about you." Brett looked at her, not sure what to expect as she continued. "He was grateful that you came to look in on him when he was sick that last time."

Brett wasn't much for taking credit for things. He preferred being perceived as a laid-back, carefree man rather than the nurturing person he actually was.

He shrugged off Olivia's words, saying, "Hey, he didn't have anybody, and he'd been there to help out when my parents died in that car accident. I think Uncle Patrick would have been completely at a loss as to what to do about the funeral and—to be honest—us, if it hadn't been for Earl.

"And then when Uncle Patrick passed on," he recalled, "Earl was there to make sure that my brothers and I were okay. He told me that if there was ever anything that I needed, to be sure to come to him. I was just sixteen and determined to look after Finn and Liam. I don't have to tell you that I was pretty damn grateful that there was someone to catch me if I fell." He shrugged as if his own actions were no big deal. "I was just trying to pay him back a little."

Olivia nodded. Brett's summary was in keeping with what she knew. "Well, Mr. Robertson apparently remembered that."

There was something in the lawyer's tone that caught his attention. "Where's this going, Olivia?"

Olivia smiled, obviously happy to be the bearer of good news. "It seems that Earl Robertson left his ranch to you."

Brett stared at her. Although Forever was surrounded by ranches, the thought of him owning one had never crossed his mind. He knew that Earl had the ranch, but he'd never wondered who it would go to if the man didn't return from New Mexico.

"You're kidding," he all but whispered, somewhat stunned by the news.

"Not during office hours," Olivia replied with an exceptionally straight face.

Numb, he asked, "Did Earl say what he wanted me to do with it?"

Olivia finished the last of her ginger ale, placed the empty glass on the bar and then said, "Anything you want would be my guess. Looks like you're finally a cowboy, Brett."

He thought about the plot of land that had belonged to Earl. As far as he knew, it hadn't been worked since the man had left. For that matter, it hadn't really been worked for a year before that, either. That was about the time when the man's health had begun to take a turn for the worse. He did recall that during the man's final days in Forever, Earl had him sell off his stock. After Earl left for Taos, the place remained abandoned.

What the hell was he supposed to do with an abandoned ranch? Brett wondered.

"You sure about this?" he asked Olivia. "I've got enough on my hands just running this place." Then, in the next breath, he asked, "Can I sell it?"

"Sure. You can do anything you want with it," she reminded him. "But if I were you, I wouldn't sell it just yet. You might want to consider doing something with the spread down the line. After all, you and your brothers take turns running the bar. Can't see why you can't do the same thing with the ranch. Maybe turn it back into a working spread again. Rick told me that's what it was before Earl got sick."

Brett laughed shortly. "What the hell do I know about running a ranch?" he asked her.

"I don't know. I do know that despite that laid-back charm of yours, you're actually a very determined man, accomplishing anything you set your mind to. Learning how to run a ranch would come easy to you. Besides, you've got friends, and they're probably more than willing to pitch in and help you out.

"And," she continued logically, "if, after a while, you decide you still don't want to be a cowboy, then I'll help you locate a buyer. I'm sure we can find someone who'll be happy to take it off your hands. The property's just outside the north border of the town. Being that close, there're endless possibilities for it if ranching doesn't appeal to you. Town needs a hotel. You could build one on the property and still have enough left to have a small spread, or anything else that presents itself to you."

She leaned back on the stool for a minute, studying him. Her smile widened.

"What?"

"Just picturing you riding around your property." She cocked her head, thinking. "I don't believe I've ever seen you on a horse, Brett."

Brett began to dust off some of the bottles that hadn't been pressed into service for a while. He believed in running a relatively pristine establishment. "There's a reason for that."

"You don't ride?" she guessed.

"I don't own a horse," he corrected. "Don't have a reason to."

Her curiosity aroused, she pressed for an answer. "But you can ride?"

"Everyone can ride in Forever," he told her. "Some of us just choose not to." He stuck the dust cloth in his back pocket while he rearranged a few of the bottles.

"Understandable." Olivia slid off her stool in a single fluid movement. "Well, I've got to be getting back. Come by the office when you get a chance so I can officially show you the will. I should have the deed transfer all squared away and notarized for you in a couple of days."

Brett nodded, still trying to come to terms with what she'd just told him. Owning Murphy's was something he'd just accepted as part of his heritage. Owning property—a ranch, no less—was something he was going to have to get used to.

"Will do," he told her. And then a thought hit him. "Oh, Olivia?"

About to cross to the front door, Olivia turned to look at him, waiting. "Yes?"

He tried to make his question sound like a casual one. "What do you know about the new doc?"

Olivia smiled. "Other than the fact that Dan's overjoyed she's here, and Tina is now hopeful that she'll see Dan sitting across from her at dinner at least a few times a week?"

Brett laughed. "Yes, other than that."

"Not much," she admitted.

The new doctor had been in town for a couple of

weeks, and no one had struck up a casual conversation with her, as far as he knew.

"Dan says her credentials are impeccable, she graduated at close to the top of her class and her letters of recommendation are glowing, although I have a feeling that he would have hired her even if the letters had been only a tad better than mediocre. Right now she's staying with Tina and Dan until she can find a place of her own, and according to Tina, she's not exactly very talkative. Why?" she asked as it suddenly dawned on her why Brett was asking. "Are you interested?"

"I'm always interested in a pretty woman," he answered. "Especially when I can't figure out what she's doing here." He saw Olivia raise an eyebrow quizzically in response to his words. "Someone who looks like that doesn't just pick up and move out to the middle of nowhere."

Olivia pretended to be insulted. "Are you telling me that I'm not attractive?"

"You didn't move out into the middle of nowhere. You came looking for your runaway sister," he reminded her. "And while you were looking, you fell in love with Rick. *Then* you decided to stay. *That's* different."

Olivia considered his narrative. "Maybe she came here looking for something, too," she suggested.

"Like what?" he asked.

"That would be something for an enterprising cowboy to find out," Olivia told him with a knowing wink, looking at him significantly. "I'll see you later."

"Later," Brett echoed.

Brett paused, thoughtfully watching Olivia leave. The last part of their conversation had intrigued him more than the first part of it had, despite the fact that he had apparently just inherited an entire ranch that he hadn't a clue what to do with.

As with everything else that challenged his problem-solving skills, he pushed the matter temporarily from his mind. He'd much rather center his thoughts on the lovely, uncommunicative lady doc.

Now, there was a challenge he would more than willingly tackle.

The word *tackle* caused his smile to widen as he went about his work.

THE NOISE LEVEL in the bar that night made it difficult to carry on a decent conversation that went beyond a few simple words. As had become the habit on Friday nights, Liam and his band were providing the entertainment at Murphy's. The band was in full swing, the music all but shaking the rafters. He could just see the few knickknacks in the apartment above slowly vibrating across the floor.

Listening, Brett had to admit, if only to himself for now, that his little brother was a damn fine performer. Liam played the guitar as if it was an extension of himself, and his voice wasn't just tolerable; it was actually good.

And getting better all the time.

As far as he knew, Liam had been at this for about a year, finally finding the courage to play in front of the people he had known all his life. Fearing that his aspirations could never reach the heights he'd wished for himself, that he was good only in his own mind, Liam had even held back from playing for his own family. It wasn't until both he and Finn had all but bullied their younger brother into giving them a demonstration that

Liam had finally played for them. What began hesitantly had gone on to be a performance worthy of a budding professional—and Brett had been the first to realize that.

After a bit of soul-searching—he'd always been protective of his brothers, although the two really weren't that aware of it—Brett had been the one to light a fire under Liam and encouraged his brother to bring his band and play at Murphy's.

For now, the weekly performances were enough to satisfy the budding artist within Liam. But Brett knew in his heart that Liam wouldn't be satisfied with this level of performing forever. Eventually, Liam would want to try his wings elsewhere. To see if he could fly.

As a rule, Brett didn't much care for change, but at the same time, he understood that nothing ever really stayed the same. But that was his problem, not Liam's. He just had to make his peace with that.

He wanted Liam to do whatever it took to make himself happy.

For a moment, Brett tuned out everything else in the bar and just listened to Liam play.

"He's better than I thought he'd be."

The comment, spoken in a normal tone of voice, still managed to cut through the din and his concentration to reach Brett. Half turning, Brett looked over to his right to see the woman who had voiced her opinion. He just wanted to verify that it was who he'd thought it was.

And he was right.

And surprised. She was the last person he would've expected to be here, given what she'd implied two weeks ago. And while he'd considered coming to Dan's clinic with some bogus health complaint just to see her in action, he'd decided to hold off and see if the woman was actually staying—or if she couldn't hack it and decided to turn tail and run.

So far, the jury was out on that decision.

"That makes two of us," he told Alisha in a vague, preoccupied voice. And then he turned on his charm. It was never far from the surface. "First drink's on the house," he told her, "although I have to say, I'm surprised to see you here."

That made two of them again, she thought. "No more surprised than I am to find myself here."

"You're sleepwalking?" Brett asked, tongue in cheek, although there was amusement in his eyes.

She didn't bother answering that since they both knew she wasn't sleepwalking, and the suggestion bordered on the absurd. She didn't know just what she was supposed to say in response to something like that. Bantering wasn't her forte and, as far as she knew, Pierce had next to no sense of humor. It probably couldn't find a place for itself with his giant libido taking up so much space.

Rather than make small talk, which she had no patience with and was not very good at in any event, Alisha went directly to the heart of the matter that had brought her here to this dim little establishment with its scent of alcohol, noisy occupants and high spirits.

"I'm told you have an apartment," she said to Brett. And with those words, Forever's new physician managed to accomplish the rare feat of surprising Brett Murphy twice in the space of a few minutes.

Chapter Three

The noise level being what it was, Brett decided that he couldn't have heard her correctly. Leaning in closer, he said, "Excuse me?"

"An apartment," Alisha repeated, raising her voice to be heard above the din. Maybe that rancher she'd treated this morning had misinformed her, and there wasn't any unoccupied living quarters to be had in this town. Doubts as well as frustration began to set in. "Do you or don't you have one?"

Had she asked that question of Finn, Brett was fairly certain that his younger brother would have thought that Forever's new lady doc was hitting on him. But Brett had a few miles on him, not so much in age—he was just thirty-two—but in what he'd experienced during that time, and he knew the look of a woman who was coming on to a man. The lady doc was most certainly not hitting on him.

To be quite honest with himself, he didn't think he could accurately describe the expression he saw on her attractive face.

From where he stood, Lady Doc was an enigma, a puzzle waiting to be solved. In a nutshell, the lady was a challenge, and it had been a while since he'd been challenged.

His interest level went up several notches.

"I do," he replied, then asked, cautiously, "Are you interested in seeing it?"

Viewing the accommodations didn't really interest Alisha. As long as the apartment—probably nothing more than an oversize closet, she guessed, given the nature of this town—didn't come with a roommate, that was all that really mattered to her.

"I'm interested in renting it," she informed him in no uncertain terms. "It is for rent, isn't it?" Alisha asked, realizing she hadn't been told that one crucial piece of information.

"I thought you were staying with Dan and Tina. Did I get that wrong?"

"No, you didn't get that wrong," she acknowledged. "For the moment, I *am* staying with Dr. Davenport and his family." There was less than enthusiasm in her voice.

"I take it that's not working out for you? Living there?" he added when she didn't answer.

Brett couldn't envision either Dan or his wife making the lady doc feel uncomfortable enough to get her looking for other living arrangements. Both Dan and Tina were warm, giving people.

Maybe it was the other way around. Alisha Cordell's looks were hot enough to melt a passing iceberg at twenty paces, but for the moment, he had to admit that the woman didn't exactly strike him as being all that warm and toasty.

Alisha frowned. She didn't like being questioned or prodded. Still, if he *did* have an apartment, she couldn't exactly just walk out now, the way she wanted to. So she answered his question—but let him know that she didn't appreciate his prying into her motives.

"Not that it's any business of yours, but I feel like I'm in the way. It's not that big a place," she added when Brett continued studying her.

Brett took a bottle from behind him on the counter and poured a glass of pinot grigio, then placed it in front of her. She looked at the glass, then at him. "I didn't order that."

"I know. It's on the house."

Another good-looking male who thought he was God's gift to women, she thought, tamping down her anger. Just because the man had a killer smile—and he knew it—did he think he could ply her with alcohol and get instant results? He was about to be surprised, she silently promised the bartender.

Taking out a five-dollar bill, she placed it on the counter. "I pay for myself."

Rather than offer her an argument, Brett merely took the money and put it into the till. "Suit yourself," he told her then got back to the business at hand. "As to the apartment, if space is what you're after, I don't think you're exactly going to be thrilled with it."

"Why?" she asked.

"To be honest, the whole thing is really just one big room," he told her.

His late uncle's apartment was predominantly meant to be just a place to sleep or to get away for a few hours, nothing more. It was not intended to suit the tastes of someone who was high-maintenance, and at the moment, that was exactly the way this woman struck him. Extremely high-maintenance.

But if that was the case, what the hell was she doing

here? He sincerely doubted that a sense of altruism was what had brought her to Forever.

She surprised him by saying, "As long as I have it to myself, that'll be fine. I don't care if it's small."

Maybe he was misjudging her. He'd been wrong before—once or twice.

Her answer led him to the only conclusion he could make. "So I guess that means that you're staying in Forever?"

"For now," she qualified guardedly. Alisha didn't believe in verbally committing herself to anything, especially not in front of someone who was the very definition of a stranger.

"How long is a *now* in your world?" he asked.

"Why?" she asked, looking at him quizzically.

As far as she could see, there was no reason for Murphy to be asking her about her plans. It wasn't as if renting the apartment to her would keep him from renting it to someone else. Obviously, the man had had no plans to rent it out to begin with. There was no sign out, advertising its availability. According to the rancher who had told her about the place, the apartment had never been rented out before to his recollection.

"That's easy," he told her. "I want to know if I'm going to be charging you by the day, the week or by the month."

"By the month will do," Alisha answered, her voice irritatingly high-handed.

He couldn't help wondering if she was that way with her patients and decided that she probably was. It looked as though this angel of mercy needed a little help getting her signals right.

"You didn't ask for my advice, but I'm going to give

it to you anyway." He saw her opening her mouth to re-
spond, and he just kept on talking. "You might find it a
whole lot easier adjusting to Forever if you stop being
so formal and loosen up a little."

"You're right," she informed him stiffly. "I didn't
ask for it."

Then, because he'd stirred her curiosity and because
she did have to try to get along with these people at least
until she decided what she was going to do with the rest
of her life and where she was going to go in order to
do it, she said, "Just out of idle curiosity, exactly how,
by your definition, would you suggest that I go about
loosening up?"

"Well, for one thing, people here call each other by
their first names—just like I'm pretty sure they do in
New York City."

She really wished he'd stop smiling at her like that.
She found it annoying—and unnerving. "I don't know
what you're referring to."

"Okay." Brett tried again. "For instance, you keep
calling him Dr. Davenport—"

"That's his name," Alisha interrupted.

"It is," Brett agreed. "But so is Dan. Around here,
people call him Dan or Dr. Dan if they aim on being
extra respectful. You keep calling him Dr. Davenport,
and Dan's liable to think that you're mad at him."

That was ridiculous. "Mr. Murphy—" Alisha began
in an exasperated voice, ready to put this man in his
place—and that place definitely did not include giving
her lectures.

"Brett," he corrected, cutting in.

She didn't come here to argue, Alisha reminded herself. She came to Murphy's to try to get herself a little

organized and ultimately secure a place to stay where she could have enough peace and quiet to hear herself think. The wounds from her sudden disillusionment and subsequent breakup were still very raw, and she needed to find a place where she could heal without hearing children squealing in the background.

This apparently was her only option, and she'd learned how to deal with limits before. "Okay, have it your way, *Brett,*" she said, deliberately emphasizing his name. "Now, are you or aren't you going to rent out that apartment to me?"

Brett thought for a moment. The apartment was his hideaway, his home away from home. But since Olivia had informed him that Earl Robertson's place was now his, that meant he could stay at that ranch house if he felt the need to get away for a few hours.

Besides, if she lived upstairs, this would give him the opportunity to interact with this iceberg who needed thawing in order to get in touch with her human side. The possibilities began to intrigue him.

His eyes met hers. "I'll rent it to you," Brett replied.

She felt an uneasy quiver in the pit of her stomach, something warning her that she was taking a step she might regret. The next moment, she locked the thought away. What was the worst thing that could happen? If she decided she'd made a mistake—again—coming here, she could just apply to another practice, pull up stakes and move on. It wasn't as if this move couldn't be undone.

"Good," she replied, refusing to look away. "Let's talk terms, Mr. Murphy."

"First term is that you remember to call me Brett," he told her patiently.

This man just didn't give up, did he? "And the second term?" she asked him warily.

If there was a first term, there had to be a second one, Alisha reasoned, and she found herself definitely not trusting this man. He was far too good-looking and smooth to be someone she could trust.

Again, Alisha noted, her would-be landlord's grin grew unnervingly wider. "The second term is that you don't forget the first term."

She waited, but nothing more came. "And that's it?" she asked, still waiting for the other shoe to drop—hard.

"That's it," Brett told her guilelessly.

"And the monthly rent?" Alisha pressed, wondering if it was going to be prohibitive—at least by his standards, she silently amended.

The woman really did seem anxious to live by herself, Brett thought, wondering if it was that she was antisocial, or if there was more to it that she wasn't telling him. And just possibly, herself, he added.

"Why don't you come upstairs with me and take a look at the place first," he suggested. There was the chance that she really didn't know what she was getting into, and what he thought was small might be unacceptable to her. "If you find that you like it, then we'll discuss the rent."

"I said I don't have to see it. I'll take it."

Brett was not about to back off from this point. "And I said that I'd rather that you *did* see it," he countered.

If she was going to rent the apartment, he didn't want her turning around in a month and stiffing him for the rent because something about the place wasn't to her liking. Having her view the place just meant there'd be one less problem down the road.

"Okay, show me the apartment," she said, barely managing to stifle a huge sigh.

Brett nodded. "Knew you'd see things my way," he told her.

Alisha swallowed the retort that rose to her lips as she reminded herself that for the time being, while she was here, this man's apartment was her one and only option.

"Hey, Finn!" Brett called out to his brother from the far end of the bar.

Finn had just poured one of their regular customers a whiskey, neat, and glanced in his older brother's direction. Brett beckoned him over with an exaggerated hand gesture.

Crossing to Brett's end of the bar, Finn asked, "What?"

"I need you to take over the bar for a few minutes," Brett answered.

"Where'll you be?" Finn asked.

Brett nodded toward the woman on the other side of the bar. "I'm going to be showing Lady Doc here the apartment upstairs."

"Oh? Oh," Finn cried as the truth of the situation, at least as he perceived it, suddenly dawned on him. "Sure." If possible, his grin was even wider than his older brother's. "You take as long as you like," he said, looking significantly at the new physician.

"That is strictly up to Lady Doc," Brett informed him.

"Gotcha. You lucky dog," Finn murmured to his older brother in a tone low enough for only Brett to hear. When it came to securing female companionship, both he and Liam agreed that Brett was the master.

"Strictly business," Brett assured him.

Finn's grin grew wider still, all but splitting his face in half. "If you say so. When I grow up, I want to be just like you," he told Brett with a wink.

Brett's response was to playfully cuff him.

Growing up an only child with no siblings to share anything with, good or bad, this kind of a physical exchange mystified Alisha—and, in a way, made her a little envious, as well.

"What was all that about?" Alisha asked. She'd heard only a few words of the exchange between the two brothers.

"A misunderstanding" was all Brett seemed willing to say. His answer made no sense to her since his cheerful expression did not match his words. "C'mon. This way," he told her, leading the way to the rear of the saloon. There was a narrow corridor there that led to the restrooms on one side and an even narrower stairway on the other.

Alisha looked at the wooden staircase with its narrow steps in obvious dismay. Was that the only way to get to the second floor?

"There's no private access?" she asked.

"The original owner didn't think to build one," he told her. His uncle had always liked to take the simplest path available to him.

The din suddenly swelled, growing even louder. Alisha glanced over her shoulder at the people at the bar and sitting at the small, round tables scattered throughout the room. A thought suddenly hit her. "I have to walk through the bar in order to get to the apartment—and in order to leave in the morning?" she questioned.

He answered, pretending that she was objecting to the distance, not the location. "It's not that far from the front door to the back," he told her. "You should be able to cross it making good time."

Alisha glared at him. He was talking down to her, she thought. "I don't need sarcasm."

Brett inclined his head. "Duly noted." With that, he

began to retrace his steps, leaving her standing where she was.

Surprised, she called out to him, "Where are you going?"

"Back to the bar." He nodded toward it. "Since you're not interested in the apartment, I thought I'd get back to work."

"I didn't say I wasn't interested in the apartment," Alisha protested.

He made his way back to her. "You made it sound as if the lack of a private entrance killed the deal for you."

She hated when things were just assumed about her— the way Pierce had just assumed she would go along with his behavior in exchange for his family name. "Did I say that?"

"No," he allowed.

"Well, then, let's go and see it," she said, pointing up the stairs toward where she assumed the apartment was located.

Brett laughed, shaking his head as he got in front of her to lead the way up the stairs. "Lady Doc, you give out really mixed signals."

"Why do you keep calling me that?" Alisha asked as she climbed up the stairs behind him.

"Calling you what?" he asked as he continued climbing.

Almost slipping, she clutched on to the banister more tightly. "Lady Doc," she repeated unwillingly.

He spared her a glance, making note of the white-knuckle hold she had on the banister. Was she afraid of heights? he wondered.

"Well, aren't you a doctor?"

"Yes, of course I am." She was frazzled at this point, and it took effort not to snap.

"Then you object to being called a lady?" he asked, doing his best to keep a straight expression on his face.

She glared at his back. She really hoped that interaction with this man was going to be at a minimum. "No, of course not."

"Then what's the problem?" he asked mildly.

Maybe he was just dense, but she had a feeling that he wasn't. What he was was annoying. "For one thing, it's not my name."

"Not your *legal* name," he emphasized. "Like I told you, we're not uptight and formal here." Reaching the top of the stairs, he stepped aside on the landing to give her space. There was very little available. "Lady Doc suits you," he told her.

He was standing much too close to her, she thought, stepping to one side. Otherwise, if she took a breath, her chest would come in contact with his, and that was completely unacceptable.

"Dr. Cordell suits me better. What?" she asked when she saw the expression on his face.

"I think Lady Doc is a better fit, at least while you're here."

"Fine, just show me the apartment so I can write you a check and get this over with." She gestured toward the closed door. "Why don't you people have a hotel here?" she asked. All this could have been avoided if she could have just rented a room at the start of this whole venture.

He shrugged carelessly. "Haven't gotten around to building one."

"I noticed that."

He pretended not to notice that she was being sarcastic now. "You might have also noticed that Forever isn't exactly a tourist attraction. Most people who pass through here pass through here," he underscored. "Those that come for a visit usually stay with the people they're visiting. Having a hotel here wouldn't exactly make wise business sense."

Turning the knob on the door that led into the apartment, he pushed it open.

"Doesn't that have a lock?" she asked, stunned. She was accustomed to apartments that came equipped with triple locks on their doors.

"It has a lock," he replied, gesturing at it.

"With a key?" she emphasized through clenched teeth. Why did she have to spell everything out? Was he slow-witted, or did he just enjoy getting her annoyed?

"Ah, well, that's another story."

"Does it have a happy ending?" she asked.

He laughed. "There's a key around here somewhere. I just have to find it."

And most likely, make a copy of it, she thought. He'd probably think nothing of coming into the apartment—with her in it—in the middle of the night. "Better yet, once I rent this, can I get a locksmith in here?"

"Do you have a locksmith?" he asked her innocently.

"Don't you?" she asked incredulously.

Just exactly what did this town have by way of services?

"Nope." He saw her rolling her eyes and waited until she stopped. "We have a handyman, though."

Alisha searched for inner strength. "Does he change locks?"

"I'll have to ask him."

"Do that," she said pointedly.

"Then you're going to rent this?" he asked.

Did she have a choice? "Is there another apartment in this town?"

"No."

Just as she suspected, she was back to having no other options. It was this apartment, or living with Davenport and his family. She knew what her choice had to be.

Chapter Four

"Well, then, I guess you have yourself a tenant," she told Brett after a few seconds had gone by.

Saying that, Alisha took a second, longer look around the premises. The last time she'd been in living quarters of this size, she was sharing the area with another medical student.

Alisha pressed her lips together, trying to focus on the upside of the situation, such as it was. Thinking back to her medical-school existence, she supposed this meant that she had twice the room now that she had then.

However, if she compared it to the accommodations she'd had when she and Pierce had lived together after they'd gotten engaged, well, then that was a whole other story. Coming from money, he'd resided in a Park Avenue apartment that was bigger than the clinic and Murphy's put together. The walk-in closets were bigger than this apartment.

You could have still had that—if you didn't have principles—and a soul.

Ultimately, she had no regrets over her decision to break it off with Pierce. If he felt free to cheat on her while they were engaged, nothing would change once they were married—for that matter, they might have just gotten worse. She'd made the right move in that situation. She just wasn't all that sure about the move that had brought her to this backwater town.

"Having second thoughts?"

Brett's question wedged its way into her train of thought. Alisha blinked, rousing herself and pushing aside memories that she no longer wanted to have any part of.

Turning toward him, she said, "Excuse me?"

"Second thoughts," Brett repeated. "You had a strange look on your face just now, and I thought that maybe you wanted to change your mind about renting the apartment."

He certainly couldn't blame her if she did. He imagined that, coming from where she did, she was accustomed to far better accommodations. There was a manner about her that didn't strike him as belonging to a struggling former medical student.

"No, I'll take it," she told him. This was better than nothing, and she really did want to have some time to herself.

"You haven't heard the rent yet," Brett reminded her.

She shook her head. "Doesn't matter. I'll take it—although I doubt if you're going to charge me very much," she added, slanting a glance at him.

Walking into the space for the first time, she took a long, hard look around. Was it her imagination, or did the place seem smaller each time she did that?

"You weren't kidding when you said it was small," she commented.

"The last owner, my uncle Patrick, didn't spend much time up here. Just used it for sleeping, mostly. There's

a combination stove, sink and refrigerator over there."
Brett pointed to a multipurposed appliance that stood
against the opposite wall. It was a faded white, but he
knew for a fact that it was still fully functional.

Alisha walked over to it, an expression of faint disbelief on her face. "Is that what this is?" She'd never heard
of anything like that before. "And it really works?" she
asked skeptically.

"It really works," he assured her, turning on the faucet to prove his point. Shutting the faucet off, he then
switched on one of the two gas burners adjacent to the
sink. Instantly, a hypnotic blue flame leaped up as if
on cue. Lastly, he opened the door below the sink/stove
to show her the interior of the refrigerator. "What did
you think it was?" Brett asked, shutting the door again.

"I don't know," she answered honestly. "Some cre-
ative toy meant for a child playing house would have
been my best guess." Looking around, Alisha realized
that there was a very crucial piece of furniture missing. "There's no bed."

Brett's smile contradicted her. "There's a bed," he
said.

It wasn't as if they were standing in a huge loft and
she'd somehow missed it. "An invisible bed?" she countered.

Rather than answer her, Brett went over to the closet
on the opposite wall and opened it. Just as he did, she
crossed to it, thinking that perhaps he was about to lead
her into another room. The next thing she knew, Brett
was grabbing her and pulling her to one side.

"What the hell are you—"

Alisha didn't get a chance to finish voicing her in-
dignant question, as the bed that had been upright and

hidden behind the closed door came flying down. Its four feet landed with a small thud on the wooden floor, part of it taking up the space where she had been standing just a moment ago.

Stunned, she found herself staring at a bed, comforter and all.

"Just keeping you from being smashed by your Murphy bed," Brett answered as if she had just asked a perfectly logical question in a normal tone of voice.

The fact that he was still holding her didn't immediately register. Her eyes widened as she turned her head to look at the bed that hadn't been there a minute ago.

"A what?" she asked, referring to what he'd just called it.

Damn, but she felt soft and round in all the right places for such a compact woman, Brett couldn't help thinking.

"A Murphy bed—no relation," he quipped. "Some people call it a hideaway bed."

"Just how old *is* this place?" she asked.

"Old," he allowed. "The saloon downstairs has been renovated, but I didn't see a reason to do anything up here since it really wasn't being used very much."

Suddenly aware that the man was much too close to her for her comfort, Alisha turned to look up at him, blanketing her vulnerability with bravado and doing her damnedest to ignore the rising heat she felt. "Is anything else going to come flying out at me?"

"Not that I know of," he replied. A laugh punctuated his words.

"Then I guess you don't have to go on holding on to me."

Her tone was cool and authoritative, meant to cover

up the fact that just for a split second, she was reacting to this closer-than-necessary contact between them. Reacting in the very worst possible way. Her body temperature had gone up, responding to his before she could forcefully shut everything down.

She'd already been this route before and learned a valuable lesson. Men who looked like Pierce—and Brett—weren't capable of maintaining lasting relationships. They were far too enamored with themselves to spare the time for anyone else.

She didn't need to bang her head against that wall twice, she silently reminded herself.

"Oh, I can think of a whole lot of reasons to hold on to you, Lady Doc," Brett told her with a smile that was half wicked, half arousing. "Reasons that have nothing to do with falling Murphy beds."

She needed to draw her lines in the sand *now,* so no mistakes could be made. "If you value hanging on to your limbs, *Brett,* I'd forget all about those reasons if I were you."

She expected another dose of his charm and was surprised—and relieved—when Brett raised his hands in an exaggerated fashion, breaking the physical contact he'd established, and took a step back.

"Whatever you say, Lady Doc. I've never forced my attentions on a woman yet, and I'm not about to start at this late date," he assured her. "I wouldn't have grabbed you now, but if I hadn't, that bed would have landed right on top of that pretty little head of yours. You're welcome, by the way."

"Thank you," she said stiffly. "I'll write you that check now." As she took out her checkbook, another question suddenly occurred to her. This time, she looked around twice before asking, "Where's the bathroom?"

Brett nodded toward the entrance of the room and the stairs just beyond. "You passed it downstairs."

He obviously didn't understand, she thought. "I mean the one that goes with this apartment."

"You passed it downstairs," Brett repeated.

Her jaw almost dropped. "There's no bathroom up here?" she cried.

"Not that I know of."

"Didn't your uncle have to relieve himself?"

"I'm sure he did," Brett replied. "When he did, he went downstairs."

That still didn't solve the problem. Just how backward were these people? "What about bathing? Didn't he bathe?"

"As a matter of fact, he did," Brett answered, taking no offense at her tone. "That's why he built a small room onto the back end of the men's room—so he could take a shower there."

Part of her couldn't believe she was actually having this conversation. "Is there one like that in the back of the women's bathroom?"

Brett shook his head. "Was no reason for it. Uncle Patrick never got married."

Alisha felt as if she'd somehow fallen through the rabbit hole without realizing it. In an odd sort of way, she wanted to see just how far this would all go. "I can't go into the men's room to shower."

"Don't see why not as long as there're no men in it. The place is pretty empty until about two in the afternoon or so, and it doesn't really get going until about five, six o'clock," he told her. "Listen, if you like, I can see about having Clarence bring a cast-iron tub up-stairs. But you've got to remember that it's going to take up most of the available space in the apartment," he warned her.

"Clarence?" Who was named Clarence these days? she couldn't help wondering.

"He took over running the hardware store after his dad retired," Brett answered. "The man's an absolute wizard with coming up with ways to get things that you need."

Alisha laughed shortly to herself and murmured, "How about a brand-new start?"

"You need a new start?" Brett asked her, interested. "Why?"

She'd said too much, Alisha thought. That wasn't like her. She waved away his question as she moved around Brett, anxious to get back downstairs to the shelter of the smoke-filled room and the anonymity provided by the wall-to-wall noise.

Turning on her heel, she started to leave. Brett caught her by the arm, anchoring her in place.

Now what? she thought.

The question he'd just put to her still hung in the air, unanswered. "I don't know how much experience you have with little bars like mine—or any bars, actually." His opening line caught her attention, and she turned around to put him in his place for whatever *knowing* thing he was about to say.

Brett continued as if he didn't notice that this new-comer was about to give him a piece of her mind.

"But when you're in a bar," he told her, "the bar-tender is like your best friend, your father and your father confessor all rolled up into one. And, also like the confessional, what is said to a bartender in confidence stays in confidence. At least that's always been my rule," Brett stressed. "People find that it helps them cope with whatever is bothering them if they know they can unburden themselves without any consequences." Brett looked at her significantly. "I don't judge."

Now, there was a new line, she thought. She could almost see how he would be successful, getting to women, having them open themselves up while they looked into those eyes that all but sparkled with some kind of mischief.

Taking a breath, she proceeded to shoot him down— or so she thought. "Number one, I don't have a best friend. Number two, my father's been dead a long time, and number three, I haven't made use of a priest since I don't know when."

Actually, she did, she silently amended. The last time was when her father had died. There'd been no solace, no consoling her grief. God had taken her father all too soon, and listening to a sympathetic-looking priest telling her that we had no way of knowing God's reasons for doing things just wasn't good enough for her.

However, she wasn't about to share any of that with this complete stranger. She had a fatalistic feeling that somehow, if she did, if she took Brett Murphy at his word, it would all wind up blowing up on her, or it would come back to haunt her when she least expected it.

Keeping her own counsel was the best way to go in this case. In every case.

But Brett, obviously, couldn't seem to take a hint, she thought in frustration. He'd taken her words of dismissal and twisted them around to indicate need.

"All the more reason to make use of me, Lady Doc. I'm here. Use me."

Desperate, her eyes flashed as she tried to make him back off one last time. "Look, I'm sure that all the women in this town would love to have you say that to them, but I am just not interested in what you're selling." She couldn't make it any clearer than that—and she didn't want to cause a scene or completely alienate him because she did want that hole-in-the-wall that he called an apartment. At least until she figured out what she wanted to do with the rest of her life.

"Not selling—offering," Brett corrected, then added, "Friendship," before she could put her own meaning to his words and light into him again. "I think you could use a friend."

So now he was clairvoyant? He was claiming to see into her heart, was that it? She was fairly certain that she had buried her loneliness better than that.

The man was probably just shooting in the dark, nothing more.

"Do you, now?" she asked, tossing her head in a studied movement of nonchalance.

He would have had to have been deaf not to pick up on her mocking tone, but he ignored it. Something told him he'd struck a nerve. Something had made her answer Dan's letter and come here, and it wasn't selfless dedication. He'd bet the saloon on that.

"I do," he acknowledged amicably. "Never knew anyone who couldn't use a friend."

"Then prepare to be astounded," she informed Brett.

He wasn't about to push himself on her in any capacity, but that didn't change the fact that he still felt he'd gotten it right. The woman needed a shoulder to lean on—and maybe to cry on once she trusted him. But that was for later, he decided.

"Have it your way," he said easily. "But the offer's still there if you ever change your mind."

Her eyes met his, and the sarcastic retort that rose to her lips died there without making it to the light of day. Maybe, in his own way, Brett was trying to make her feel welcome. For now, she gave him the benefit of the doubt.

"I won't," she told him quietly. "Now, how much do you want?"

They'd just been talking about friendship—at least he was. Her question seemed to come out of left field. Brett shook his head slightly, as if to indicate that something had been lost in translation. "For?"

"The apartment," she cried. Wasn't the man listening at all? "How much do you want in exchange for renting out the apartment to me?" she asked, carefully specifying everything so there wouldn't be any further confusion—or whatever it was that he was feigning.

"You're still interested?" Brett asked incredulously. He'd been fairly confident that not having a bathroom or shower on the same floor as the bedroom would have sent her hurrying off into the night.

"*Interested* is probably too positive a word in this situation," she granted. "But it is what it is, and I do want to have some peace and quiet and *privacy*." She underscored the last word intentionally, hoping that got the message across to her new landlord. Once she was inside the apartment, she wanted to be left alone. "There's very little of either in Dr. Daven—in Dan's house," Alisha amended, catching herself at the last moment.

Why she felt it was necessary to go along with what Murphy had cited as the *terms* of their agreement was really beyond her. After all, the man would have had to have been crazy to declare the rental agreement null and void if she referred to the doctor by his occupation coupled with his surname.

On second thought, she reconsidered, looking up into Murphy's eyes; maybe he *was* a little off-kilter. Just off-kilter enough to want her to live up to that ridiculous term he'd given her—or else. Who rented out a box of a place without a bathroom and still expected to be compensated for it?

Well, he thought, the woman definitely knew what she was getting into. There were certainly no hidden surprises to spring on her. She'd seen the place, for better or for worse.

Grinning, Brett put out his hand. "Works for me," he told her.

Alisha looked at him and then down at his hand. She shook it almost hesitantly.

"It's my hand, Lady Doc," he prompted, "not a rattlesnake. Don't be afraid to shake it."

That goaded her enough to firmly grasp his hand this time and shake it the way she would have if a sane person had offered her his hand to shake.

"Okay, now do you have papers for me to sign?" she asked.

Every rental agreement she'd ever known or heard about came with legal papers to sign—and notarize, most of the time. He hadn't said anything about that, or standard things like first and last months' rent.

An uneasiness whispered along the fringes of her mind. Just what was she getting herself into? a little voice in her head whispered.

"No," he replied guilelessly.

She stared at him, confused. "What do you mean, *no?* Don't we have a deal? Or did you suddenly just decide *not* to rent the apartment to me?"

Now that she thought about it, it would seem in keeping with the man to just jerk her around like this. There was obviously a lack of entertainment in this town, at least from what she'd witnessed so far.

"We most certainly have a deal," Brett told her, nodding at the hand that she had dropped to her side. "We just shook on it."

He *was* jerking her around, Alisha thought. "I don't understand."

Maybe she didn't, Brett decided. Glancing toward the bar, he saw that Finn seemed to be holding his own serving the customers. That cleared the way for his taking another minute or so to explain things to this beautiful tenderfoot who had been sent their way.

"Around here, we seal our deals with a handshake," he told her.

Yeah, right—sure they did. They couldn't be that naive—could they?

"And that's enough?" she mocked.

"Shouldn't it be?" he asked her seriously. He felt sorry for the world she had come from, where trust seemed to be such a rare commodity. "If a man's—or a woman's—" he amended in case she was the type to take offense at what she perceived was a slight "—word isn't good enough, then there's no point in entering into any kind of an agreement with them, because they'll break a contract just as easily as they'll break their word."

"The difference being is that lawyers can make you live up to a contract." Didn't he realize that?

Brett smiled a rather unfathomable smile. "They can

try," he corrected. "Depends on where you are. Lawyers are only as good as the respect they command—and that involves their word, and whether or not they keep it."

Another argument that wouldn't be going anywhere, Alisha thought wearily. As a last sarcastic gesture, she took out her handkerchief and waved it in the air in front of him.

Brett merely nodded, the corners of his mouth curving significantly. "I knew you'd see it my way."

"I didn't exactly have a choice," she said pointedly.

The corners of his eyes crinkled. "I guess you didn't," he acknowledged in the nicest tone she'd heard in a very long time.

Chapter Five

"There," Alisha said, ripping out the check from her checkbook and handing it to the man on the other side of the bar. "Two months' rent," she added, confirming what they had just agreed on.

Quoting a nominal amount as the rent, Brett had initially requested only one month. Since it was so low, she had insisted on paying him for two—just in case, in that amount of time, she hadn't made up her mind about remaining. It gave her some leeway.

Alisha had taken a seat at the end of the bar in order to write the check out. Finished, she put her checkbook away and started to get off the stool.

"If there's nothing else…" she said, her voice drifting off, her meaning clear. If he didn't want her to sign a lease or anything of that nature, then she was leaving.

Brett put a hand on hers to keep her seated for a moment longer. She looked at him quizzically. "Wait—you can't leave yet."

Now what? Alisha thought uneasily. Had he realized that he'd charged too little? "Change your mind about the amount?" she asked.

When he'd quoted her the amount for the rent, she thought he was giving her the weekly figure, not the monthly one. Even though the apartment was so small, he was renting the place out for way too little, in her opinion. She kept that thought to herself.

Even as she wrote out the check, Alisha had a feeling it was going to suddenly dawn on her new landlord that he could get more for it, even though it was little more than coffin-sized. Granted, she was accustomed to the astronomical rents in New York City, but she had a feeling that what he was asking for was low, even for a tiny Texas town.

"What?" Belatedly, he replayed her words in his head. "No, the amount's fine," he reassured her. Brett planned on putting whatever checks he received from her into an account earmarked for repairs and future renovations for Murphy's. It seemed like the only fair thing to do since, as far as he was concerned, this was an unexpected windfall.

"Then why's your hand on mine?" She looked down at it and then up at him, waiting for a reasonable explanation as well as a withdrawal of that same hand.

Rather than raise his hand away from hers, he lightly drew it back, his fingers ever so softly sliding along the length of hers.

The crackle of electricity that sizzled between them was hard to miss. He had a feeling she was thinking the exact same thing. Only difference, he mused, was that she wouldn't be willing to admit it. Given half a chance, he would.

"I thought we'd have a drink, celebrating your new quarters and our new relationship," he told her in his best Southern-gentleman drawl.

"Our relationship?" she echoed incredulously.

What was he talking about? There was no relationship. Had she made a mistake, renting this apartment?

A nervous restlessness began humming through her. At the very least, she needed that handyman he'd mentioned to come by and install a dead bolt—provided the man knew what that was, she added with a note of weary despair. She was beginning to think she'd set up camp at the end of civilization.

"Landlord and tenant," Brett replied, indicating first himself, then her. "Why? What did you think I was referring to?"

Still sitting on the stool, she squared her shoulders. "I didn't have a clue," she lied. "That's why I asked."

Brett nodded toward the collection of spirits behind him. "You want something light and fruity—or something hard?" he asked her.

The words seemed disconnected as they came out of the blue like that. Confused, she could only ask, "What?" as she stared at him.

"To drink," Brett prompted. "Light and fruity—" he gestured toward the small array of bottles filled with colorful mixed drinks "—or hard?" he concluded, waving a hand toward the bottles that contained alcohol his customers downed straight.

She shook her head to both choices. "Nothing, thanks. I need to get going."

"The evening's young, and so are you," he told her with a grin that insisted on corkscrewing right into the center of her chest. "One drink to toast the apartment— and your settling in Forever. Just our way of showing how very welcome you are," he added. Before she could turn him down, he said, "The town's not exactly growing by leaps and bounds, but we're still wearing Dan out. You came just in time to save him—and us." There was the underlying sound of amusement in his voice. She couldn't tell if he was being serious or not.

She still hadn't made up her mind about this town and its inhabitants. She'd come here because it was somewhere to go in order to get away. But now that she was here, she had to rethink the idea of remaining in town for any length of time, never mind about *Forever*. That wasn't even on the table at the moment.

After a beat, she realized that he'd stopped talking and was looking at her with the most soulful, knee-melting eyes she'd ever encountered—and that included Pierce's, whose eyes, until this moment, had held the record for being able to make her melt in an astonishing amount of time.

But she'd been in love with Pierce, which partially accounted for her reaction to him, Alisha silently argued. She certainly wasn't in love with Brett Murphy.

As a matter of fact, she sincerely doubted she was even *in like* with the man. As far as she was concerned, he rubbed her completely the wrong way. Lord knew, she'd had her fill of men who *knew* they were seductive, complete with bedroom eyes, and used that so-called *talent* to get whatever they wanted.

So what exactly did Brett Murphy want?

"One drink isn't going to hurt anything," Brett coaxed her.

She supposed that he had a point. A single drink *wouldn't* hurt anything.

Putting her purse on the counter, she said, "All right. I'll have a Long Island Iced Tea." When he didn't ask her what that was—as she'd half expected him to—she said, "How much?" Opening her purse, Alisha took out her wallet.

"Put your money away," he told her. "It's on the house." With that, he began mixing the drink.

Rather than do as he'd said, she took out several bills. "Oh, no, I want to pay for it. I don't like being in someone's debt."

"If anyone is in anyone's debt," he told her seriously, "the town's in yours—for coming to help Dan and making it so that he can take a vacation without feeling like he was abandoning us." Finished, he set the drink down on the bar in front of her.

Without thinking, she automatically drew the drink over to herself. Her mind was on what Brett had just told her. A cold chill ran down her spine. She'd never been the only doctor in charge before. At the hospital, there'd always been a multitude of seasoned physicians to turn to, veteran physicians to use as a sounding board if something was unusual. The thought of being strictly on her own was *not* a heartening one.

"Vacation?" she repeated. "He didn't say anything about a vacation."

Her voice had gone up slightly. It wasn't exactly panic he heard, but it wasn't the last word in confidence, either. He hadn't meant to rattle her. At least, not about her work. If he was going to set her pulse racing, it would be with a whole different goal in mind. Fear wouldn't have been part of the equation.

"Don't worry. Knowing Dan, he's not going to leave you until he thinks you can fly solo for a week…or two," he added more quietly.

"Or two?" Her eyes widened as she struggled to get her nerves under control. She'd be treating colds and hangnails and aching muscles, just like she had been these past two weeks under Dan's tutelage. How hard could it really be?

She still couldn't quite manage to get her uneasiness to subside completely.

Brett gave her his most reassuring smile. "He's not pushing you out of the plane until he knows for a fact that you can open the chute."

"Do all your pep talks involve being airborne?" she asked, redirecting her edginess to focus on Brett rather than her own uneasiness.

Brett lifted a shoulder and let it drop in a careless shrug. "Seemed to fit the occasion, seeing as how the look on your face was as white as a parachute," he commented. "And technically, even if Dan does go on vacation, you won't be alone," he assured her.

"Don't tell me you studied medicine on the side, between mixing drinks."

"I won't tell you anything that's not true."

The way he said it, with his eyes holding hers, cut through the layers of doubt, distrust and sarcasm, going straight for softer territory. She could almost believe that he was being truthful.

Almost.

"Then you'd be the first man to do that since my father," she replied quietly.

"Heady company," he commented, inclining his head. "I'll be sure to act accordingly." With that, he raised the glass he'd poured for himself, indicating that she should follow suit. When she did, he said, "To the beginning of a beautiful friendship."

Then, because the evening had settled into a comfortable rhythm, his brother doing, in his opinion, very well without him, he lingered, adding, "And to you, Lady Doc, for coming to tend to our wounds and our ills."

With that, he downed his drink. She took a sip of

hers, then regarded it thoughtfully for a moment. "What did you just have?" she asked, nodding at his empty shot glass.

"Wild Turkey, 101 proof," he told her.

She pushed her glass to one side and said, "I'll have the same."

Brett looked at her uncertainly. "Are you sure?" he asked. "It's rather strong, and you might get more than you bargained for."

Her eyes locked with Brett's. "I think I already have."

Because something told her that this man was going to be there, around her, at every turn, in spirit if not in the flesh, she needed to show him that she could go toe-to-toe with him if need be. And that she wasn't about to become one of the worshipful cluster she was certain he availed himself of from time to time, when the whim hit him. She had no wish to blend into a crowd.

"The Wild Turkey," she prompted, looking at the bottle that was back among the others on the counter behind him.

Taking a double shot glass, he put it on the bar in front of Alisha and poured a serving accordingly. "Your call—" he began.

Before the words had left his lips, the whiskey had gone past hers. She had thrown it back in one fluid movement.

The smooth liquid blazed a trail of fire all the way down her throat and into her stomach. She felt it reaching all her limbs almost simultaneously.

Returning the shot glass to the counter, she looked at him unwaveringly, silently informing him that she was up to any challenge he threw her way.

Whether or not that was true was another story entirely.

Her eyes weren't tearing up, Brett noted, relieved. That meant this wasn't her first go-round with the potent alcohol and that her bullheadedness hadn't gotten her in too deep.

He'd misjudged her. And he had to admit, he was somewhat impressed.

"Want another?" he asked, waiting to see what she'd say. If bravado had been her intention, she would have asked for another. But she didn't—which impressed him even more.

Moving the drink he'd previously poured for her back in front of her, Alisha said, "I'll pass." A touch of humor curved her mouth. "I need to stay clearheaded. After all, I might be on call if there's a three-horse pileup on Main Street."

He studied her for a long moment, trying to make up his mind about her and realizing that in order to do that accurately, he was going to need more input. Maybe a lot more input.

"Why'd you come here, Lady Doc?"

Her eyes narrowed. "I thought we just settled that. To rent the apartment you have upstairs."

"No, I mean, why did you come to Forever?" he specified.

"Daven—Dan told you that. I answered his open letter. He said he sent it to half a dozen teaching hospitals— I was the only one who answered him."

Brett knew all that. Even if Dan hadn't told him, there were hardly any secrets in a town the size of Forever. But that wasn't what he was asking her.

"Why did you *really* come?" he asked. "And don't

give me any altruistic pap," he added with another sensual smile that ultimately made it difficult for her to get angry at him.

"You don't think I'm altruistic?" she questioned.

Some of the alcohol must have gotten to her, Alisha surmised, because this was where she should be taking offense—and she wasn't. But she was surprised that she managed to be that transparent to this bartender/confessor.

"Oh, I'm willing to believe that you're altruistic enough," Brett allowed. "But that's not the reason you're here." He leaned in across the bar, dropping his voice so that only she could make out his words, which seemed only right, seeing as how they were meant for only her and no one else. "What are you running from?" he asked her quietly.

She knew she should be angry at his assumption, both that she was running from something and that he had a right to ask as well as a right to know. But she was struggling with shutting out the warm, aroused feeling that had washed over her when his breath had touched her cheek as he spoke.

Alisha did her best to block out everything, both the good and bad. "What makes you think I'm running from anything?"

The lady doc had just proved his point and didn't realize it, he thought. "Because you didn't say no, that you weren't."

"No, I'm not," she replied firmly with a toss of her head. The movement brought with it the hint of a headache, a bad one, in the making. Damn, what did he *put* in that whiskey? she wondered. She usually didn't get strong headaches after having just a single drink, even if that drink was strong enough to dislodge blasting caps a quarter of a mile away.

Brett looked unconvinced at her belated protest. "Sorry—it doesn't count when I have to prompt you," he told her.

"You're not prompting me," she denied vehemently, then stubbornly insisted, "And I am *not* running." She waited a beat before adding, "I'm walking."

"From?" he asked gently, giving every indication that he could wait until the second crack of eternity for her answer, if that was what it took.

Oh, what did it matter? Maybe saying it out loud would help purge her of all this anger. "From a rich, self-centered bastard who thought that just because he had relatives who smuggled themselves on board the *Mayflower,* that meant he could do whatever he wanted to whomever he felt like—and I would be patiently waiting in the wings for him to come back."

Brett unscrambled the rhetoric rather quickly. He'd heard it all before. Not quite in those terms, but he'd definitely heard it before.

"He cheated on you."

"Apparently with the immediate world," Alisha bit off.

He went a little further out on the limb and made a guess. "You were married to him?"

"Oh, please," Alisha protested with an exaggerated expression of disdain as she rolled her eyes. "I was engaged to him," she corrected before she realized that she was laying herself bare before this smooth bartender. She never went on like this—*ever*. She looked into her now-empty glass as if she'd find some clue at the bottom of it. "Damn, what did you lace this drink with? Sodium Pentothal?"

"Gotta plead not guilty to that one. I'm fresh out of truth serum," he told her. "All I've got at my disposal is a bartender's willingness to listen."

"Or a bartender's willingness to pump the new kid on the block for information," she corrected.

Brett laughed softly, shaking his head. "No pumping. Just a willing ear," he reminded her. "So what happened to the cheating bastard you were engaged to? I don't picture you as the type to let him get away with it."

This had gone way beyond any of his business. This was the part where she knew she should just stand up, tell the man she would be moving in tomorrow morning and then walk out.

That was what she knew she should do.

It wasn't what she did.

The reality of it was that she remained sitting on the stool. Sitting there and telling this imperfect stranger what had been festering within her and eating away at her for the past month.

"No, I didn't let him get away with it," she replied. "I threw my engagement ring at him, told him it was off and told him where he could permanently take up residence. I also," she added with relish, "told him not to pack suntan lotion because he was going to fry anyway."

Now, *that* he could see her doing. The guy deserved it, he thought. He had to have confetti for brains to go wandering off, bedding other women when he had someone like this woman waiting for him at home.

Brett laughed. "Remind me never to get on your wrong side."

"You've already come close a couple of times," she

informed him, wrapping both hands around the empty glass as if to anchor herself to something.

"I'll keep that—" *and you* "—in mind," he told her amicably.

He was smiling at her—so why did she suddenly feel as if she'd been put on notice?

"Okay, I'll be back in the morning to move in," she told him.

"I'll be here," he promised.

"I figured that," she replied.

In Brett's opinion, she didn't sound all that happy about his presence. It was going to take a bit of work, but he and the lady doc were going to find some interesting middle ground, he promised himself.

Alisha slid off the stool and slowly tested the strength of her legs—just in case. Despite having knees that felt a little wobbly, her legs were just fine.

She left the saloon without a backward glance. Even so, she could have sworn she felt Murphy's eyes on her, watching her all the way to the front door.

And even after the door had closed, even though she knew it wasn't possible.

Chapter Six

"So? What was that all about?" Finn asked. The moment the door closed behind Alisha, Brett's brother made his way over to his brother's side of the long bar. "Saw you and that new lady doctor raising your glasses and toasting something. Anything I should know about?"

Brett saw at least three regulars close to him leaning in, ready to hear anything he had to say. He deliberately moved to the side and lowered his voice before answering. "I just rented out Uncle Patrick's old room."

Finn looked at him in surprise. Following his brother's lead, he turned his back to the men at the bar. The noise level and Liam's band took care of the rest. "I didn't know we were looking to rent it out."

"We weren't," Brett replied. Taking her empty glass and the two shot glasses, he made his way over to the sink to wash them out. "It was her idea."

"I thought she was staying with Dr. Dan and his wife."

Finished, Brett picked up a dish towel to dry the glasses before putting them back near the liquor bottles. "She was."

This obviously wasn't making any sense to Finn. He

liked having things spelled out. "They get into some kind of argument or something?"

Based on what she had shared with him, Brett had his doubts about that. "She didn't mention that, just said she wanted her own space."

Finn laughed shortly. "She's not getting much more than just a *little* of it. Does she know there's no bathroom up there?"

One of the customers at the bar raised a hand to attract his or Finn's attention. No more communication was necessary than that since he knew what Max Keller drank. Clan MacGregor whiskey without fail. Picking up a bottle of the whiskey from the counter, he made his way over to the man.

"She knows," he told his brother.

Like a dog with a bone, Finn followed him around, asking questions. "And she's okay with that?"

Brett shrugged as he poured two fingers' worth into Max's glass. "I think *okay* is stretching it a little, but for now, she's willing to go along with using the facilities down here."

Moving away from Max, Brett turned and looked at his brother thoughtfully. They were all, perforce, handy when it came to small fixes and doing what needed to be done, but Finn had a real talent not just for taking things apart and repairing them, but for building things from scratch, as well.

"How long do you think it would take you to put in a small bathroom upstairs?" he asked Finn.

The question took the younger Murphy aback. "Where would you suggest I put it? That space is pretty cramped as it is."

Neither one of his brothers ever went up there any-

more and had obviously forgotten about the layout, Brett
thought. "There's the storage closet," he reminded Finn.

A light entered Finn's eyes for just a moment, then
went out again as he recalled the area. "It's full of junk."

"We can empty it," Brett said with finality, dismissing the minor problem. Leaning a hip against the bar,
he studied Finn. "So how long do you figure it would
take?"

Finn thought for a moment, then said, "Well, that depends."

Now that he'd made up his mind, Brett wanted to
nail things down as quickly as possible. "On what?"

Three new customers came in and took the last available seats at the bar. This time, Finn made his way over
to the men, and Brett followed him. "On whether or
not you've got me working shifts at the bar at the same
time," Finn answered.

"How long if that bathroom's the only thing you're
working on?" Brett specified.

Finn set out three shot glasses and deftly filled them
with an easy flick of his wrist. "I can have it done inside a week as long as I can get the supplies I need and
a little help with the demolition."

Quoting a price to the new occupants at the bar, Finn
collected the amount and rang it up at the register behind them. Finished, Finn paused, studying his older
brother. And then the familiar Murphy grin materialized. "You really want her to stay, don't you?"

There was no such thing as a completely private conversation at the bar. Brett kept his response deliberately
vague in case, despite the ongoing din, he was overheard.

"I want her stay here to be civilized" was all Brett
would commit to. "But for now, you're not working that

bathroom, so get back to tending the bar. Mind that it's the bar that you're tending and not those girls," he pointed out, nodding at the four young women who had just walked in. The women, all in their early twenties, were clustered at the far end of the bar, standing because there were no available stools left.

And they were all looking their way, Brett noted.

"I can do both," Finn assured him, then added with a conspiratorial wink just before he moved down the bar, "Hey, I learned from the best."

Brett merely waved him on, making no comment one way or the other.

"Hey, I'm dying over here. What's a guy gotta do to get a drink around here?" Cameron Lewis asked.

"All you've got to do is just ask, Cameron," Brett responded, picking up a bottle of the man's drink of choice. "Just ask."

"Well, I'm askin'," the man declared.

"And I'm filling," Brett replied, pouring dark, thick liquid into the man's freshly emptied glass.

MISS JOAN'S AMBER eyes slanted toward the front door of her diner. She'd felt rather than heard it opening. There were stories that the older woman and the diner were all but one, and that she could feel every scratch her counter sustained, could literally feel the vibrations of the door each time it was opened or closed.

People who said they knew better laughed the stories off but secretly always felt there was a strong possibility that the stories might contain a kernel of truth.

Her attention shifted to the young woman who had just walked into the diner. Miss Joan still never missed a beat of the conversation she was having with two of her customers as she took down their orders. Those who understood the term knew that Miss Joan had invented multitasking long before it had become a byword for an entire generation. Moreover, the redheaded woman with the sharp eyes and sometimes sharper tongue made it all look easy.

When Miss Joan recognized who had entered her diner, she quickly disengaged herself from the people who had placed their orders. Depositing the slip with their lunch orders on the counter in front of the kitchen, she made her way over to the counter where the diner's newest customer had just seated herself.

"I was wondering when you were going to finally come here on your own. What'll it be, honey?" Miss Joan asked in a welcoming voice.

"A cup of black coffee, please," Alisha requested, never bothering to pick up the menu that lay on the table in front of her.

"And?" Miss Joan asked, waiting for the rest of the order.

"A napkin?" It was more of a question than anything else because Alisha wasn't really sure what the older woman expected to hear.

"No, what'll you have for lunch?" Miss Joan asked patiently. This one needed gentle treatment, Miss Joan had already decided when Dan had brought her around that first day.

"Oh." Alisha paused to think for a minute, doing her best to pull herself together. She'd just left Murphy's and was stalling rather than going on to where she'd been staying these past two weeks.

"Nothing. Just coffee." She was feeling unusually vulnerable right now, trying to center herself and decide just what she *really* wanted to do. She didn't feel as if she belonged anywhere.

"You can't be expected to function on just coffee," Miss Joan chided. "You need something that'll stick to those skinny little bones of yours."

One of the first things Alisha had learned upon coming to this town was that everyone eventually turned up at Miss Joan's, and that the slightly larger-than-life woman seemed to know everyone's business whether or not they told her about it firsthand. Dan had told her that although the woman blustered at times and could bark out instructions like a drill sergeant when the spirit moved her, inside that gruff, gravelly voice was the heart of a woman who could feel other people's pain and had an unending capacity for compassion and empathy.

"I don't—" Alisha began to demur, but her protest never saw the light of day. Miss Joan just took over.

Patting her hand, the older woman said, "Leave it to me, honey. I'll take good care of you." And with that, she told one of her waitresses to bring back "Today's special for the doc here."

As the girl hurried off to give the order to the diner's senior short-order cook, Miss Joan turned to face Forever's newest resident.

"How's it going?" she asked in a tone that indicated she was really interested in finding out just how Alisha was getting along. Tired, drained and trying to find the words she needed in order to tell the doctor she was working with that it was nothing personal, but she'd found new lodging, Alisha didn't have any words left over to spare.

"Okay," she replied, hoping someone would call the

diner owner over so that she could just sit here in relative peace.

"That doesn't sound very convincing," Miss Joan replied. She peered more closely at the new doctor's face as if she was making up her mind about something. "Not sleeping too well, are you?"

Alisha thought of denying the woman's assumption, then decided that there was no point in denying what was probably so obvious. There were circles under her eyes, put there thanks to children who never seemed to sleep for more than ten minutes at a time.

But, in her opinion, complaining about the doctor's children bordered on being a shrew, so she just shrugged and said, "I'm just trying to get accustomed to a new place."

Miss Joan smiled at her as if she knew better. "Tina's kids are a good bunch, but they can be a handful. They're certainly noisy enough to wake the dead when they get going," she testified. She'd babysat the trio on a couple of occasions and could speak from firsthand experience. She had a very soft spot in her heart for the children, but she wasn't blind to their energetic behavior. "But you, coming from New York City—the city that never sleeps and all that—you're probably used to constant noise in the background."

"Yes," Alisha allowed, then added, "but not in the next room."

Miss Joan surprised her by saying, "I've got a spare room at my place. I could just call and tell my husband to get the bed made up if you wanted to crash there for a while—"

She really hadn't expected that. There was more to this woman than she'd thought. "No, that's all right.

Thank you for the offer, but I've already made other arrangements."

Miss Joan looked at her sharply, doing a quick analysis.

"You're not leaving us, are you?" she asked. "I know these folks take some getting used to, probably more than most new places. But if you give them a chance, you might find that you're glad you stayed. These are all good people," Miss Joan assured her, "and they'll be there for you if you need 'em. Living here is like having one big extended family. We've got our share of squabbles, no doubt about it, but deep down, we're all family."

"No, I'm not leaving," she told the woman. *At least, not yet,* she added silently.

Miss Joan nodded, taking the young woman at her word. "Good to hear," she said.

Someone called out to the diner owner, and for a second, Alisha thought her prayers had been answered and the woman would be moving on. But Miss Joan merely waved a hand at the man who'd called out to her, not even turning around. Instead, Miss Joan continued studying her.

"If you're not leaving and you're not staying with Dan and Tina, then—" Miss Joan drew out the word, and suddenly, her face grew more animated as the answer occurred to her. "If you're staying in town, then you got Brett Murphy to rent you his uncle's old room above the bar, didn't you?"

Damn, the woman *was* clairvoyant, Alisha thought. If she'd had that kind of insight herself, she might have been spared the humiliation that she'd gone through because of Pierce.

"Dan said you were very sharp," she told the older woman with a touch of admiration.

"I just pay attention," Miss Joan replied. This might get more interesting at that, the older woman thought. Her waitress returned with that day's special, a whiff of heat swirling above the plate. Miss Joan placed the dinner on the counter before the young woman. "Eat up, Doc. You're gonna need your strength," Miss Joan predicted.

Alisha didn't know if the remark referred to her work—or something else. In either case, she discovered that the scent of the roast turkey, mashed potatoes and even the peas had her appetite suddenly making an unexpected, dramatic appearance.

ALISHA COULD HEAR the noise growing louder before she ever opened the door the next morning and crossed the saloon floor.

Hammering and drilling.

With a vengeance.

The bulk of her worldly possessions were in a storage unit back in New York City. What she'd taken with her was divided up between the two suitcases that she'd hastily packed when she was leaving. She had one in each hand now as she made the significant transition from house guest to renter.

The bar looked empty inside.

"Hello?" she called out.

The door to Murphy's had been unlocked, but once she stepped into the cool darkness, she didn't find a single Murphy around. She thought that was rather strange since she'd told Brett that she was moving in today.

She'd taken a few hours off from the clinic to get settled in. When she'd told Dan and his wife that she was moving to her own quarters—and assured them that it wasn't anything they had done that had her leaving— they had been incredibly understanding and kind about the matter. It had almost made her feel guilty about leaving—but she did want a little peace and quiet in her own space, no matter how small it was.

Except that the words *peace and quiet* really didn't seem to have a place here. Not with all that noise practically making her teeth vibrate.

"Hello?" Alisha called out again, louder this time. Louder or not, she still got the same results. The only thing answering her was the hammering and the drilling.

What was going on here?

As she crossed the floor and went to the rear of the building, the noise, dovetailing and then blocking each other out, grew louder still. It seemed to be coming from upstairs.

Her upstairs, she thought. She'd paid two months' rent; that entitled her to throw out whoever was making all this racket.

Tough talk for a peanut.

That was what her father had always said whenever she would lose her temper about something. The words were always laced with affection, but they did bring her attention to the fact that she was not exactly an imposing figure. It also encouraged her to control her temper whenever possible.

Squaring her shoulders, Alisha began to go up the stairs, a suitcase in each hand.

At this rate, she was just going to toss her suitcases

on the floor and make a hasty retreat, hoping that eventually, whatever was happening up here would stop.

And if the noise didn't subside by tonight, she was going to demand her money back and—

And what? Crawl back to Dan's and ask him if she could move back into the guest room? She couldn't do that. It would be too embarrassing. Sure, Dan and his wife had taken the news well, telling her they understood. But if she came back the same day, they'd think she was a loon. She'd be packing up for good before she knew it.

And going where?

No, for better or worse, right now she needed to stick it out in Forever. But if she couldn't, for whatever reason, settle in upstairs, then where?

Miss Joan's? She could envision the woman working on her, slowly drawing out every shred of information she had within her.

Maybe she could sleep in the clinic, Alisha thought, ruling out Miss Joan's. One of the exam rooms had been converted to a makeshift hospital room where patients who'd had nonthreatening, minor surgery stayed overnight to recover and rest. She could stay there until she figured out her next move, Alisha told herself. All things considered, it couldn't possibly be as noisy there as what she was currently hearing.

Having gone up the stairs far slower than she was happy about, Alisha marched toward what was now her apartment and set the suitcases down on the landing just outside the door. As she entered, she was about to demand to know what the hell was going on here when she suddenly had her answer.

Or at least part of it.

At the far end of the room, where there had once

been a solid wall, there was now a big gaping hole. But instead of daylight coming through, Alisha saw what appeared to be a room or something akin to one beyond the one she was standing in.

Taking a few steps into the noise-drenched area, she could feel the hammering and the drilling all but reverberating within her body.

But the increased noise was nothing in the face of what she found herself looking at. Brett and one of his brothers—Finn, was it?—stripped down to their jeans, their bare chests gleaming with sweat, each manning either a drill or a sledgehammer.

Were they ripping apart her apartment so she couldn't make use of it? After charging her rent? Why would they do something like that?

Determined to get an answer, she marched over to Brett and addressed his back in a raised voice. "What are you doing?" When neither he nor his brother turned around to answer her, she surmised that they hadn't heard her. Small wonder—she could hardly hear herself think, much less talk.

Rather than try again and vainly shout at the two men, she tapped Brett on the shoulder. She nearly regretted it the next moment when he swung around quickly, startled by the unexpected contact.

As he turned to face her, he held the hammer he was wielding aloft so as not to accidentally hit her. "Morning," he said brightly.

Morning? Was that all he had to say while he was destroying the place she was supposed to be staying in? Was he some kind of maniac?

"What are you doing?" she shouted at him. Her voice

all but echoed around the space because Finn had turned off the drill.

"What does it look like?" Brett asked cheerfully.

"Like you're ripping the place apart," she accused, trying very hard not to notice that the man had a very tempting rock-hard body, and that it was hardly *inches* away from hers.

"Close," Brett acknowledged. "We're building you a bathroom."

Chapter Seven

"A bathroom?" she repeated, fairly certain she wasn't hearing Brett correctly.

Alisha had an uneasy feeling that the sight of all those hard ridges along his bare chest and incredibly flat stomach was interfering with her ability to process information properly. Moreover, she was having a great deal of difficulty tearing her eyes away from his torso. It was only with a concentrated surge of effort that she managed to raise her eyes to his face.

For once, Brett wasn't wearing that sexy, cocky grin, she noticed with relief.

"You're building a bathroom up here?" Alisha questioned in disbelief. Just like that? He hadn't mentioned anything last night. Last night, he'd made it sound as if the facilities downstairs were her one and only option.

Brett nodded. If he was aware that he was somewhat underdressed for this conversation, he gave no indication.

"After giving the matter some thought, it didn't seem right charging you that money without throwing in a basic facility." He nodded toward his brother—also underdressed, she couldn't help thinking. "Finn's pretty handy with tools, so I figured we'd give getting this bathroom in place a shot."

That was all well and good, but meanwhile, Alisha thought, she had this gaping hole in her apartment, which negated the whole idea of *having* this apartment in the first place.

"And where am I supposed to stay while this is going on?" she asked. *Look at something else, 'Lish,* she told herself, realizing that her eyes were once more riveted to his gleaming upper body. *Look at anything else.*

Easier said than done.

"Here," Brett told her, answering her question. "Finn's building the bathroom in what used to be the saloon's storage room. It's not going to interfere with your living here."

The hell it won't, she thought. Alisha looked at the gaping hole again. Maybe she could hang a drape or tape newspapers over the opening as a temporary fix.

But seeing as how they were doing all this without forcing her to either bargain for a bathroom or pay for it, she didn't think she had all that much right to complain about the inconvenience or the noise. To do so would seem rather small-minded and petty of her in the face of the Murphy brothers' generous gesture.

Forcing herself to look elsewhere again, she murmured, "That's very nice of you," to Brett. "Of both of you," she amended, realizing that she was leaving out the man Brett had just indicated was in charge of the remodeling. She could only pray he knew what he was doing.

Finn slanted a look in her direction, acknowledging her recognition, then got back to work. Within seconds, the noise as well as the heat was once again enveloping the room—and her.

The noise was coming from the tools. The heat, however, came from another source and was proving to be far more dangerous to her peace of mind. The heat was being generated by Brett's and Finn's bodies as they worked. Muscles tensed and bulged, and their bare chests gleamed with sweat that seemed to be just cascading off their tanned upper torsos.

She needed to leave. To find somewhere with cooler air, somewhere where she could breathe. The air in what was now her apartment was suddenly in dangerous short supply.

"I'd better get to the clinic," she heard herself mumbling.

Brett stopped swinging his hammer, resting it on the floor before him. There were beads of perspiration all along his brow. Alisha found herself curling her fingers into her palms to keep from reaching up and brushing his perspiration away.

"What?" he asked, resting on the shaft of the sledgehammer. "I'm afraid I didn't hear you."

"The clinic," she said, pointing vaguely in the general direction where she assumed the squat, one-story building was situated. "I should be getting to it." *And away from here before I do something incredibly stupid I won't forgive myself for.*

Brett's brow furrowed beneath the damp hair plastered on his forehead. "I thought you said you were moving in this morning."

"I am. I did." She pointed toward the two suitcases in the doorway. She'd intended to put their contents away and make herself at home a little. But she definitely couldn't do that now, not with Brett here like this.

"That's it?" he asked, surprised at how little she'd brought.

Alisha thought of her things, all neatly tucked away in the storage unit halfway across the country.

"I travel light," she said, not bothering to mention the rest.

"Lighter than any woman I've ever met," Brett readily acknowledged.

He hefted the hammer again, ready to resume swinging. The demolition part was very nearly finished. Then came cleanup—but right now, that wasn't his problem. He had to be getting downstairs to get ready for the day's work soon.

"I'll see you later, then," he told her.

"Later," she echoed, nodding her head as she began backing away. Taking a breath, she swung around to face the doorway and quickly vacated the premises, driven away not by the noise but by the spine-melting sight of two half-naked men. Two very impressively built half-naked men. Heaven knew she'd never seen anything in anatomy class that came close to what she had just been privy to. Certainly never anything that had her pulse revving up and launching into double-time the way that it was currently doing.

It felt cooler to her the moment she got to the landing.

Alisha just kept going without a backward glance.

"Everything all right?" Dan asked when he saw his new associate hurriedly throwing on her white lab coat and then slinging her stethoscope around the back of her neck.

"Fine," Alisha answered a bit too quickly.

Dan gestured for her to come in. He closed the folder

he'd been making notes in and pushed himself back a little from his desk to study his young associate. "I thought you were going to be settling into your new quarters this morning."

"I'm settled."

"That quickly?" he marveled. He looked at her more closely.

"I didn't have much," Alisha reminded him, then added, "And I didn't want to hang around and get in the way."

"In the way?" he echoed, puzzled. "In the way of what?"

She realized that she'd managed to miss a button on the lab coat and began to undo them all. What was wrong with her? She'd seen unclothed patients before. Completely unclothed patients. But none, she was forced to admit, had ever made her spine tingle and her knees threaten to give way.

"The sledgehammer and the drill," she answered, rebuttoning her lab coat.

Dan shook his head. "I don't…" His voice trailed off, leaving his young associate room to jump in with an enlightening explanation—if she could.

"Brett and his brother—" She paused, trying to remember his name.

"Liam?"

Alisha shook her head as she took the seat in front of him. That wasn't it. "The other one."

"Finn."

Her face brightened with recognition. "Yes, that's him. Finn. Brett and Finn are adding a bathroom to the apartment."

Dan absorbed the information and smiled as he nodded. "That just might come in handy," he commented. "Listen, if you want to go back, maybe help out to make the construction go quicker, I can handle the patient load. After all, I've been doing it these last four years. A few more hours won't kill me."

An image of Brett, his chest damp and glistening, flashed through her mind. She could feel herself reacting accordingly just from the memory of him. She definitely couldn't go back to see the real thing. That was just asking for trouble.

"No, that's all right," she assured Dan with feeling. "I'd rather stay here. Besides, I'd probably just be in the way. What I know about construction could probably fit on the head of a pin—with room to spare."

"Well, you're one hell of a good doctor, and that's what really counts," he told her.

She looked at him, slightly bewildered. It wasn't that she didn't welcome the praise, but she hadn't done anything in the past two weeks to merit that sort of thing. What was he referring to?

"How could you know that?" Alisha asked. "I've only been here a few weeks."

Dan smiled. "Well, I could say that I'm a keen judge of character and that I can read things into the way you interact with the patients and what you find significant in their health histories—or I could tell you that I had your file forwarded from the hospital. It makes for interesting reading."

"You had my file forwarded?" she asked incredulously. She'd just assumed, the need for a doctor being what it was, that Davenport would have just been glad she was breathing.

He nodded. "I thought I'd save us both some time if I got to know your work through your previous efforts. That was some call you made in the E.R. with that boy. Considering all the commotion that was going on that night, according to the report, a lot of doctors might have missed that one symptom," he complimented her, referring to the fact that there'd been a telltale pink line forming around the area that had been cut, a sure sign that an infection had set in.

"That's in there?" she asked, surprised. She hadn't made a big deal of it, just made the notation in the chart and treated the young boy—saving his leg in the bargain, she'd thought with quiet pride.

"Every last detail," Dan told her. "You impressed the chief resident, and from what I recall of Gavin Stewart, that's not an easy thing to do."

Alisha stared at him. "You *know* Dr. Gavin Stewart?"

He smiled at her. "Actually, he interned under me," he told her.

"Small world," Alisha marveled. Suddenly, she wasn't quite the outsider she'd been a few minutes ago. They had something in common now beyond their choice of a profession.

"Not as small as Forever," Dan said, seeing the humor in the situation.

"Doctors," Holly Rodriguez said, sticking her head into Dan's cubbyhole of an office. Her expression was serious, but not alarmed. Very little alarmed the steadfast young woman. "Marlene Ryan's here with her son, Zack. I think he's got a broken arm. Marlene said Zack was trying to be a bronco buster like his dad. Apparently, the horse had other ideas."

"Looks like we're on again," Dan said, pushing his chair back even farther and rising to his feet. Alisha was quick to follow suit.

IT WASN'T UNTIL more than ten hours later that the clinic was able to close its doors, allowing Alisha to drag her tired body back to Murphy's.

Too tired for dinner, she'd passed on both Holly's and Dan's separate invitations to join each for dinner with their respective families.

All she wanted to do was fall face-first on her bed—provided she could get it to stay down—and sleep until she had to get up again for work tomorrow.

But as she approached Murphy's, she couldn't help wondering if she was going to be subjected to the construction noise that she'd heard going on this morning. However, at this point, she had her doubts that it would keep her from sleeping. She was *that* tired.

Mercifully, she didn't detect any drilling or hammering when she opened the door to the saloon and walked in. Only the sound of voices, mostly male, raised in boisterous conversation.

A good many of the men were lining the bar. She moved past the patrons like a woman in a semitrance, totally unaware that as she passed, she was garnering looks that varied from mildly interested to borderline lecherous.

The latter was quickly squelched by a glare from Brett, silently putting the offending parties on notice. Brett ran an orderly establishment, which both men and women felt comfortable frequenting.

"Lady Doc," he called to her as she passed him. "How was your day?"

"Long" was all Alisha trusted herself to say as she kept walking.

"Need a little something to help you unwind?" Brett inquired.

From where she was, it sounded more like a suggestion. Dog-tired though she was, Alisha recognized that beneath the exhaustion, she was pretty wound up after the lengthy day she'd had. She didn't remember sitting down after Holly had announced the first patient, which meant that she'd spent more than ten hours straight on her feet.

Retracing her steps back to Brett, she asked, "What would you suggest?"

He had a feeling she didn't realize that she'd just asked him a loaded question. Even tired-looking, Alisha Cordell was a damn gorgeous woman. He had a great many answers to her question that really couldn't be voiced in public, or even really suggested in private, not at this juncture of their acquaintance.

But there was no denying that he did find himself exceedingly attracted to her, and if and when conditions were right, he intended to act on that attraction—but not yet and not now. The town needed another doctor more than he needed to explore tempting new regions, no matter how much he wanted to. He did not want to be responsible for scaring her away.

Brett had to admit, though, that this was the first woman he could recall who had tempted him to this point since Laura Wellington had left Forever—and him—in her rearview mirror.

To date, Laura had been the only woman he'd ever wanted to marry. The only woman who had made him temporarily forget his responsibilities. He found his loyalties torn and his resolve waffling. What had finally made up his mind for him was Laura herself—but not in any way she had intended.

His parents were gone, and his uncle had just died, leaving him to fend for himself and his two younger brothers. Laura couldn't wait to kick Forever's dust off her feet, and she wanted him to come with her. The moment they graduated high school, she'd been hell-bent on taking off. When he hesitated, she had given him an ultimatum. He had to choose: it was either her or his brothers. At fourteen and thirteen, they would have been turned over to become wards of the county.

He couldn't do it, couldn't let that happen. He chose his brothers, and Laura took off, permanently fading out of his life. He'd hurt some, then just shut down that part of him. Pining away was for people who didn't have a living to earn, and he'd had three of them to provide for.

That was in the past now, and in all that time, he hadn't found anyone he'd been willing to give his heart to. While he had dallied with and enjoyed many women since then, none had ever interested him, had ever moved him, the way that Laura had. He'd been fairly convinced that no one ever would.

And then Alisha Cordell had come into town.

Where the hell had all that come from? It wasn't like him to drift off like that. Especially with someone waiting on him. Lady Doc was obviously waiting for him to answer her—after all, he'd been the one to engage her, not vice versa.

"I've got a drink right here," Brett told her, reaching beneath the counter for a bottle he had set aside just for her, in case he could interest her in having a social drink before retreating to her apartment.

The saloon was fairly dim, but there was enough light coming through to filter through the bottle, casting a rainbow of lights.

Alisha eyed the bottle suspiciously. "That's not going to knock me for a loop, is it?" she asked the bartender.

"No loops involved," Brett guaranteed. He crossed his heart for good measure. "It's just going to loosen all those clenched—muscles of yours," he finally concluded with a knowing smile that, despite her best efforts, immediately undulated beneath Alisha's skin and worked its way throughout her entire being in approximately sixty seconds flat. "Ultimately allowing you to relax," he told her.

"Fine, I'll take it to go," she said in all seriousness.

Brett shook his head. They were relatively lax in Forever, but there were some rules they had to follow. "Sorry, it has to stay down here. It won't take you long to finish the drink," he promised. "It's not all that potent."

The drink he served her was pink and foamy, fizzing and sprinkling the skin on her hand as he poured. "What do you call it?" she asked.

"How about the Lady Doc Special?" Brett suggested, trying the name out for size. "Seltzer, strawberry liqueur and a dash of valerian root and chamomile to help you relax. The locals swear by it."

The man had an endless bag of tricks, she thought. "Works for me," she told him. Had she just said that in her head—or out loud? At this point, Alisha really couldn't be all that sure.

Picking up the glass, she tentatively sampled it. It

was fruity and smooth and very light on her tongue. She liked it instantly.

"It's good," she said in surprise.

"I thought you might like it," he said with satisfaction.

The next moment, as he watched, the object of his interest downed the drink he'd concocted rather faster than he'd thought she would. But as he'd just told her, there was nothing harmful in the drink, just some flavored soda water and a few natural herbs.

The herbs were a natural relaxant that would allow her to get the sleep she so desperately needed. He didn't want the noise from the bar, muted though it was by the time it reached the apartment, to keep her awake, even for a little while.

"Thank you," she said, putting the glass down on the bar. As an afterthought, she told him, "Put the drink on my tab."

Then, with measured, deliberate steps, Alisha made her way to the rear of the building, the staircase being her goal.

She counted the stairs as she went up each one, a rather hypnotic alternative, in this case, to counting sheep. Her eyes threatened to shut on her before she reached the landing. Alisha found she had to struggle with them to keep them open.

Finally reaching her door, she unlocked it, went inside and carefully relocked it again. Three steps inside the apartment had her standing in front of the door behind which her bed resided.

With one swift, calculated movement, she pulled open the door, moving quickly to the side in order not to have the bed come down on top of her.

The bed crashed down.

A second later, she crashed down on it.

She was asleep the moment her face touched the squashed pillow.

Chapter Eight

Alisha had always considered herself to be a light sleeper.

She was easily roused by any undue noises, and she had managed to also train her subconscious to wake her if she had to be on call by a certain time. This ability, to wake up within a couple of minutes of the time that she *needed* to be up, came in handy when she'd been an intern, then a resident at Faith Memorial Hospital.

But uncharacteristically, for the first time in a very long time, these past seven hours she'd slept like a dead person. It was a deep sleep where she heard nothing, dreamed nothing, almost as if she had fallen into some sort of suspended animation.

Ultimately what had woken her up was the smell of coffee.

At first, she thought she was finally dreaming. But if that was the case, the aroma would have faded once she was awake.

It didn't. It only grew stronger.

Sitting up and focusing, Alisha half expected to see a coffeepot on that combination appliance thingy that Brett had pointed out to her when he'd initially shown her the apartment.

But there was no pot of coffee on the stove, no cof-feemaker going through its paces on the minuscule counter, either.

Was the smell of coffee coming from downstairs? She didn't recall Brett saying anything about coffee brewing at Murphy's.

Still sitting there, now fully awake, Alisha stretched, trying to pull her thoughts together and put them in their proper perspective.

Then it actually hit her. She'd slept through the night. The *entire* night.

Since she never did that, she could only attribute it to the drink that Brett had given her with the natural sedative. But she didn't feel groggy. If anything, she felt refreshed.

And *really* craving that coffee she smelled.

Alisha swung her legs off the bed at the same time that she realized she hadn't changed last night but had fallen asleep still dressed in her clothes.

Glancing down, she saw how wrinkled they all were. "Nice fashion statement, 'Lish," she upbraided herself out loud.

Dragging her hand through her hair, she thought for a minute and actually debated marching downstairs to use the shower. Brett had told her she could do that, but she would have felt a great deal better about showering in the men's room if she had some kind of a lock for the bathroom door, a lock that belonged exclusively to her. She felt very uneasy contemplating using the one that Brett had installed on the door downstairs. What if someone suddenly materialized with a key and walked in on her while she was taking a shower?

The people she'd interacted with at the clinic so far

all seemed rather nice, and she was fairly certain that her privacy was safe with them, but she was a long way from knowing *all* the people in and around Forever, and she had never been one to leave things to chance—especially not when it came to something as personal as taking a shower *privately*.

Alisha was still debating her next move when she heard a knock on the door.

"It's me, Lady Doc. Brett," he said, identifying himself in case she didn't recognize his voice. "You decent?"

"Yes, I'm decent," she told him. "And wrinkled," Alisha murmured under her breath, frowning down at her clothing.

"Can I come in?" he asked.

She glanced over toward the door. Since he wasn't trying the doorknob, that meant he didn't have a copy of the key he'd given her.

Either that, or he was just trying to give her a false sense of security so he could come in on her unannounced when she least expected it. He seemed nice, she admitted, even though he was a great deal sexier than she was comfortable with, but he hadn't fully earned her trust yet. She needed more than just *nice* and certainly a lot more than just *sexy* before she could give someone her trust.

She sighed. She was dressed, so having him come into the room didn't matter to her one way or another. "Sure," she told him. "Come on in."

She waited. Several beats passed, and he still hadn't come in.

"Are you coming in or not?" she asked.

"You're going to have to open the door for me," he

answered. "I had Clarence come in and change the locks the way you requested, remember?"

She remembered talking to Brett about it, but she hadn't realized that he had gone ahead and called in the handyman.

Sliding off the bed, Alisha crossed the half dozen steps it took to reach the door. With each step that brought her closer, the scent of coffee only seemed to get stronger.

When she flipped the lock and finally opened the door to her apartment, she saw why. Brett was carrying a tray in his hands. A tray with a large tumbler of coffee and a bright blue plate with breakfast on it. Eggs, bacon and white toast.

"I thought you might like breakfast to get you started your first morning here," he told her.

Her stomach growled, reminding her that she hadn't eaten for a while, but she refrained from reaching for the tray. Had he made that here?

"Dan told me that you and Miss Joan have this arrangement where she doesn't serve liquor, and you don't serve food."

"I don't serve food," he acknowledged, placing the tray on the small table.

Like the rats enticed by the Pied Piper's flute, she followed the food to the table. "Then what's this?" she asked, gesturing at the contents on the tray.

"That's my *bringing* food to a friend," he pointed out. "There's nothing in that agreement that says I can't cook food for me and mine."

Unable to keep herself in check much longer, Alisha removed the plate from the tray, putting it on the table and the tray on the floor.

"And I fall into that category?" she asked. Alisha didn't know if she found that concept confining—or rather comforting and nice.

"You fall under 'miscellaneous' for now," he corrected. "I live a few doors down from here," he explained as he watched her sit down at the table. "I like to cook breakfast, and I figured you might be hungry since you didn't have any dinner."

"How would you know that?" she asked, surprised—but not as surprised as she would have been two weeks ago. People in this town seemed to know things about one another, things that people in a much larger city didn't bother knowing—or finding out.

Brett took no affront at her tone. He'd probably be spooked, too, coming in from the big city where no one trusted anyone else. "You'd be surprised how fast word gets around in a small town like Forever. Not too many secrets here."

"I wouldn't think whether or not I ate dinner the night before would be something that would fall under the heading of *secrets*. Personally, I just think it's too trivial a fact for anyone to take any note of."

Brett laughed. She probably had a point. "There's also not all that much to do in a town this size. You wouldn't believe what passes for entertainment around here.

"Anyway," he said, changing the subject back to what he was originally saying, "I was making breakfast for myself, Finn and Liam, and I thought maybe you'd like to have some, too."

At this point, her senses all but being assaulted by the tempting smell of the food that Brett had prepared and brought in with him, she was far too hungry to pretend she wasn't.

Murmuring her thanks, she made short work of what was on the plate, and she washed it down with the coffee he'd brought.

The first long sip had her eyes all but widening to their full capacity—and then some.

"Wow, I could have really used your coffee when I was an intern." Eighteen-hour shifts would have been a snap with this black brew running through her veins, she thought.

"Too strong?" he questioned.

She laughed shortly. Boy, was *that* an understatement.

"*Too strong* is too weak a term for what's in here. Who taught you how to make coffee, someone in the asphalt business?" she asked wryly.

"My dad," he told her. "He used to work two jobs, going from one to the other and getting very little sleep at all." He nodded at her coffee. "He'd drink that to keep him going."

"Keep him going?" she echoed. "Drinking this, it's a wonder the man managed to close his eyes. Ever," she emphasized. Even so, she consumed half of its contents before she set the tumbler back on the tray. Alisha sighed, feeling rather full. "What do I owe you for this?" she asked.

His expression was unreadable. He had the ability to turn that off and on at will, she realized, feeling just a touch frustrated because she couldn't tell what was on his mind when he assumed that expression.

"Did I tell you I was charging you for breakfast?" he asked.

"No," Alisha began, but got no further in her response.

"Then you don't owe me anything," he concluded. "By the way, I got you a lock," he told her, placing the item on the corner of her tray, then putting down the accompanying keys. He saw her look up at him quizzically. "The lock's for when you take your shower in the downstairs men's room." She glanced over toward where the hole in the wall had been and discovered that it was covered by a makeshift drape hammered, not hung, into place. "It's going to take Finn a few more days to finish your bathroom," he explained, an unvoiced apology implied in his tone. "After he's done, you won't have to worry at all about someone walking in on you at an inopportune time."

She laughed. He was being thoughtful, and she really wanted to believe it was on the level. But she'd been fooled by a good-looking guy acting thoughtful at the outset of their relationship—big-time. She didn't want to be the fool again.

"With you second-guessing all my needs," she said with a touch of sarcasm in her voice, "you make it hard to leave Forever."

"That is the general idea, Lady Doc," he told her in a moment of honesty.

"Oh?" Did he mean that on a personal level, or was he speaking for the town?

"We don't want you to leave."

Never one to show all his cards, Brett resorted to using the all-inclusive pronoun, but what he was really referring to was himself. He was beginning to realize that *he* didn't want Alisha to leave. At least, he silently insisted, not yet. Not until he decided just how attracted he was to this woman and where that attraction would lead him—if it went anywhere at all.

Picking up the tray from the floor, he slid the plate and tumbler onto it. "Well, I'll let you get to your day. I've got to get to mine," he told her, and then, for no apparent reason he could think of, he added, "I told my brothers I was taking them to inspect my new property this morning."

"You bought some property?" There was obviously more to this man than was evident at first glance. Was he a businessman with his eye on expansion? Or was he referring to a strip of land somewhere, purchased to satisfy the inner cowboy within him, something she was beginning to suspect existed within almost every male in Forever?

"No," he said, wanting to set her straight. "Seems I inherited this chunk of land."

Now that she looked more closely at him, Brett didn't seem to be too happy about coming into the property. That meant that he'd been affected by the passing of whoever had left him the land. Sympathy flooded through her before she could think to stop it.

"Oh, I'm sorry," she said quietly. "Did someone close to you die recently?"

Since her voice was full of sympathy, it caused Brett to wonder just how many times she had dealt with that very same question, or been in a position to offer condolences to a friend or family member of a patient who hadn't been able to survive whatever had brought them to the hospital in the first place. She looked as if she actually was sincerely sorry.

"He died recently," Brett replied, "but he really wasn't close to me."

She watched him, puzzled. His answer didn't make

any sense to her. "Then why did he leave you his property?"

Brett moved his shoulders in a vague, dismissive shrug. "Because I was nice to him and not too many people, it seems, were."

There was more to it than that, Alisha judged. People didn't write wills if the disposal of their possessions didn't matter to them. Whoever had left the property to Brett had a definite connection to the bartender.

"Funny, you don't look like a Boy Scout," she quipped.

The sly curve of his mouth was back. That moment of vulnerability she'd glimpsed was gone. "That's 'cause I'm not."

No, Alisha decided, studying him, Murphy was probably the complete antithesis to a Boy Scout unless she'd totally missed her guess. But there *was* something there, beneath the charm and the smooth talk. He had his walls, and she had hers. Walls came in all sorts of different configurations.

But at bottom, that was his business, not hers, she reminded herself.

"Thanks again for breakfast," she told him as he walked across the threshold.

"Don't mention it."

Brett turned around for a moment to say something else, but she had already closed the door. He heard the lock flip into place. His mouth curved at the corners. It was going to take a lot to win this one over, he mused, going back down the stairs with his tray.

He'd always liked a good challenge.

THE DRIVE TO the property that Earl Robertson had left to him was a relatively short one. The ranch was located just at the edge of Forever. Olivia had come by yesterday to give him the deed, which she'd had transferred to his name.

It was official. The ranch was now his.

Brett brought his car to a stop before the gate. It, like the fence on either side of it, was all but falling apart. Weather and termites had been at it relentlessly over the past few years.

After getting out, he pushed the gate open, then looked over his shoulder at the two occupants still in the car. Finn, as always, rode shotgun. Liam, all but in his own world, most likely writing another song in his head, Brett assumed, was in the back.

"Well, don't just sit there—come on out," he told his brothers.

Finn and Liam got out on either side at the same time. Neither one looked thrilled about being dragged out to view the deserted ranch.

"I thought you wanted me to finish that bathroom," Finn reminded his older brother.

"I do," Brett responded, "but this isn't going to take long."

He took a long look around. It had been a while since he'd been up here. Nothing seemed to have changed, he noted. There was still a cool breeze here, despite the fact that the temperature was climbing.

"I have that practice with the band," Liam spoke up.

"I know. Like I just said," Brett repeated patiently, "this isn't going to take long."

"Don't see why you need us out here anyway. It's not like we know anything about ranching," Finn pointed out. He had his interests and his strengths, neither of which included overseeing a spread or having anything to do with horses.

"Well, neither do I," Brett replied.

He surveyed the field they were in. It was green and lush and perfect for cattle to graze on. In the five years since Robertson had okayed the sale of his herd, the land had had time to recover and flourish—not that he knew very much about ranching beyond that. But he knew potential when he saw it.

"So this is yours, huh?" Liam asked, scanning the area and actually taking it in for the first time. "Not too shabby."

"Ours," Brett corrected. Both brothers looked at him quizzically. "This is *ours,*" he emphasized in case his brothers had somehow missed his meaning.

Finn looked at him uncertainly. "I thought you told us that Olivia said old man Robertson had left this land to you."

"He did," Brett confirmed. Then, before either brother could ask more questions, he said, "What's mine is yours." Brett looked from one brother to the other. "You know that."

Finn flashed him a wide grin. The family resemblance was always strongest when they smiled like that, Brett thought.

"Does that sharing principle apply to that cute lady doc, as well?" Finn asked.

Brett's tone was one of tolerance. It had taken him a while to develop that particular quality, but it had evolved out of necessity. He wouldn't have been able to survive rearing his brothers without it.

"She's not mine," he informed Finn.

Finn, apparently, thought he knew better.

"Yet," Finn corrected. "She's not yours *yet.* But I saw the way you were looking at her the other morning when she came in while we were working on the bathroom—the one you decided she needed," he underscored, his meaning clear: Brett was not as indifferent to the woman as he was pretending. "Hell, brother, it's just a matter of time before that woman is another notch on your belt."

"Or your bedpost," Liam, not to be left out, added.

Brett shook his head. "When are you two going to grow up?" he asked in exasperation.

Finn gave him a knowing look. "Probably around the same time you hang your hat on one bedpost—for good," he replied.

He didn't have the kind of time that a relationship like the one Finn was alluding to required. There were still too many things left for him to do.

"Not going to happen for a long time," Brett promised a shade too quickly, as if he wasn't at ease allowing the suggestion to hang there between them.

Finn exchanged looks with Liam and grinned broadly. "Then I guess little brother and I are going to stay young like this for a long time to come."

Brett snorted as he walked around the field, stopping to check out the soil at random. "Since when does your action depend on what I do or don't do?"

"Since you became our idol and role model, big brother," Finn told him with a very straight face, under the circumstances.

"Maybe I should have come out here alone after all," Brett said. "It's not often that I get the chance to find peace and quiet away from you two lunkheads."

Finn turned to Liam, feigning seriousness. "I think he hurt my feelings."

Liam nodded with feeling, getting into the spirit of the thing. "I know he hurt mine."

"Ha! You two don't have any feelings," Brett countered. "You both have hides like rhinos." He gestured toward his car and began walking back to it. "Now shut up and get back into the car."

Liam appeared all too ready to comply and quickly turned back, picking up his pace, changing it from sluggish to fast. "We're going back?" It was a rhetorical question.

The next moment, Liam was shot down.

"No, not yet," Brett told him. The news was met with less-than-overwhelming enthusiasm. "We're going to drive around for a bit, get the lay of the land the way it is now and then go see how much repair the main house is going to need."

Reaching the car, Finn pulled open the door and got in. "In other words, more work."

"In *any* words, more work—eventually," Brett replied, getting in himself.

Maybe inheriting this property was going to turn out to be a good thing, he mused. It would certainly bring them closer together as a family, the way things used to be when they were younger—as long as he succeeded in getting his brothers in gear.

Chapter Nine

"You're next, Millie," Holly Rodriguez announced through the large rectangular opening that looked out onto the medical clinic's waiting room. "Dr. Davenport will see you now."

Millie Edwards, the woman whose name had just been called, rose from her seat. But rather than head toward the door that would lead her to the rear of the clinic, where the examination rooms were located, the middle-aged homemaker approached the desk where Holly was seated. The nurse was inputting information into the clinic's brand-new computer, purchased just for this very function.

Millie stood there quietly, waiting for Holly to finish what she was typing.

Sensing her presence, Holly paused. Her fingers rested lightly on the keyboard as she looked at the older woman.

"Is something wrong, Millie?" she asked, seeing the somewhat hesitant expression on Millie's almost wrinkle-free, round face.

Millie stood with her back to the rest of the occupants in the waiting room. Lowering her voice to almost a hoarse whisper, she said, "No, but, um, would it be all right if I just wait for the other one? The lady doctor?" Millie asked hopefully.

"Sure," Holly told her, taking care to keep the smile from her lips.

She glanced at the list and called out the name of the next person on it, a big, burly man by the name of Jake Horn, who had just taken over running the local feed store for his uncle.

Jake shuffled past Millie, nodding a general greeting toward her.

"It's not that I don't like Dr. Davenport. I do," Millie said nervously to the doctor's nurse once Jake had gone through the door. "But, um, this is a lady problem and, um..." Embarrassed to even be mentioning what had finally brought the harried mother of three over to the clinic, Millie's voice slowly trailed off on a helpless note.

"It's all right, Millie," Holly assured the woman. "Dr. Dan wants you to be comfortable when you come to the clinic."

"But I don't want to hurt his feelings—or insult him," the woman added, her eyes widening as the last thought suddenly occurred to her.

"Don't worry about it, Millie. Dr. Dan doesn't take offense easily. You're just exercising a patient's right to pick and choose their primary physician," Holly told the woman diplomatically.

Millie still looked unconvinced. "You're sure he won't be insulted?" she asked uncertainly.

"I'm very sure," Holly told her with gentle finality. "Now take a seat, and as soon as Dr. Cordell is ready, I'll send you in to see her," she promised.

Several minutes later, Holly saw Zander Cruz emerge

from exam room 1. After pausing to make a payment on his bill, the man entered the waiting room and then headed for the clinic's front door. That meant that the new doctor could see the next patient.

But rather than send Millie in immediately, Holly rose from her chair and made her way back into the rear of the building.

Alisha looked up as she heard someone coming into the exam room she was currently in. But instead of the anticipated next patient, she saw the clinic's nurse standing in the doorway.

"We can't be out of patients, can we? Or are you my next patient?" Alisha asked, finding the idea mildly amusing.

Holly laughed softly, shaking her head. "Unfortunately, we're definitely not out of patients. It's almost standing room only out there, but I just thought you might want to know something."

"Oh?"

The single word carried a note of leeriness in it. At this point in her life, after her fiancé fiasco, any surprises coming her way were suspect and unwelcome.

"Your next patient is Millie Edwards—and I thought you'd like to know that she specifically asked for you." Holly smiled as she delivered the news. "I believe that makes Millie your first official patient by choice in Forever."

Alisha had been seeing patients for close to three and a half weeks now, but to her knowledge, this was the first one to actually request her—choosing her over the clinic's resident physician.

Alisha's eyes crinkled as she smiled at the nurse,

appreciating the notification. "Thank you for letting me know."

Holly returned the smile. "My pleasure, Doctor. I'll send Millie in now."

Alisha nodded. "Please." She watched Holly leave the room.

She hadn't thought it would matter that much to her, being singled out by a patient and having that patient actually request seeing her, but it did. So much so that Alisha felt as if every fiber of her being was smiling.

Big-time.

The feeling lasted for the rest of the day, weaving its way into the late afternoon and the beginning of the evening—even when fatigue set in.

"WELL, YOU CERTAINLY look happy," Brett noted as his one and only tenant walked by the bar later that evening.

The crowd along said bar had thinned out somewhat since the doors had officially opened a little after noon and the "late" shift—people coming in after they'd had their dinner—hadn't begun to pour in yet. Occupied as usual, Brett had still been watching the front door, waiting for Alisha to come through it on her way to her apartment.

He'd found himself keeping an eye out for her every night now, whenever he was on duty—and of late, he was on duty every night, at times sharing the job with one of his brothers, at times going it alone. Liam, devoting himself more and more to nurturing his musical career, played with the band at Murphy's at least two nights a week, if not more.

Finn lent a hand at the bar far more often than Liam did, but the truth of it was, his middle brother was predominantly busy with making renovations to the ranch house that he had insisted belonged to all of them. The upstairs bathroom had been completed, as Finn had promised, within a little more than two days of Alisha's moving in.

His brothers, Brett thought with pride, each had a special talent. His lay in keeping the family together no matter what.

The sound of Brett's voice burrowed into her thoughts, and Alisha looked at her too-good-looking-for-her-own-damn-good landlord for the first time, mildly surprised that she was inside Murphy's. These days, she'd discovered, she came here almost by rote, as if she was on some sort of automatic pilot.

Tonight she'd stopped to have dinner with Holly at the diner where the latter used to work until she'd graduated from online nursing school. Holly had done that just after she'd married Ray Rodriguez, the last of the eligible Rodriguez brothers.

Miss Joan had served them dinner personally, and for once, Alisha noted with relief, the titian-haired woman had been too busy asking Holly questions to grill her—that meant that she'd gotten a pass for the evening.

Alisha had to admit, though, like everyone else in the town, she was growing fond of the eccentric woman. Miss Joan had truly missed her calling. The woman should have been an interrogator for one of the alphabet agencies. She was rather confident that Miss Joan would have worn down just about any suspect who crossed her path.

Not quite ready to pack it in and call it a night just yet, Alisha drew closer to the bar and leaned in. "I'm sorry—I didn't catch that. What did you say?"

For his part, Brett drew in closer, as well. Only a few inches separated their faces. A fact that he had a feeling they *both* noticed.

"I said you looked happy. It's a nice look on you," he commented. "Any particular reason you're currently giving off more light than the sun?" he asked, the corners of his mouth curving not just in humor, but in deep appreciation of the way she looked, as well.

In his opinion, Alisha Cordell was a woman who owned every room she walked into whether she knew it or not, but when she smiled like that, she wasn't just beautiful; she became incredibly stunning.

"In case you haven't noticed, it's nighttime," Alisha pointed out. "The sun's not up anymore."

Brett never missed a beat. "But if it was, it definitely would retreat in the face of the competition it would find itself dealing with, having you beaming like that. Want to tell me what's up?" he asked. And then, just as suddenly, a thought occurred to him as to why she might be looking as happy as she was. "You're not about to go back to New York, are you?"

The question was playfully stated, but he wasn't altogether surprised that the thought of her leaving bothered him. He'd just gotten used to seeing her around, used to looking forward to seeing her walk out each morning and walk in each night. He was reluctant to face that coming to an abrupt end.

"No, not now," she said with feeling. "I'd be leaving Dan in a lurch."

Alisha appeared unaware that her referring to the doctor by his first name had been noted—with a surge of satisfaction—by the man she was speaking with. She was coming around nicely, Brett thought.

"Someday," she interjected, not wanting Brett to think she was in any way contemplating becoming a permanent resident of this one-pickup-truck town, "but not right now."

"Okay, so what *has* you smiling from ear to ear?" he asked, adding, "You might as well tell me, you know. Resistance really is futile. We bartenders are known to be relentless when it comes to extracting information."

Settling in without fully realizing it, Alisha perched on the closest bar stool. "Someone asked for me at the clinic today. Specifically. They wanted me to attend to them, not Dan." She was doing her best not to sound or seem smug, but it really did feel good, she couldn't help thinking.

Brett paused to study her face, and then he laughed, shaking his head.

"Wow, if that was all that it took to get you to smile like that, I would have come into the clinic your first day there and asked for you. Specifically," he underscored, finding himself totally captivated by her dazzling smile.

"That wouldn't have counted," she told him, dismissing his comment with a wave of her hand.

"Why not?" he asked, pretending to take offense at the rejection.

She sighed. Okay, she'd spell it out for him. "Because you wouldn't have meant it. You would have just been doing it to be nice."

Brett paused to get a couple of glasses, then poured her a drink first. Moving the drink in front of her, he dispensed a glass of beer for himself, only half filling it.

"How do you know that?" Brett asked, his eyes locking with hers. "How do you know I wouldn't have meant it? How do you know I wouldn't have actually wanted to see *you* instead of Dan?" he challenged softly.

Alisha had a flippant remark all set and ready to go on the tip of her tongue. It wasn't exactly a put-down so much as a verification that she knew he would have just been trying to build up her confidence—he seemed to have a knack for looking into her soul and supposedly *seeing* things about her she was unaware of. It was something he had referred to as a *good bartender's gift.*

But her remark, well-intentioned or not, never emerged because Brett's liquid green eyes had all but taken her prisoner, seemingly looking deep within the recesses of her soul, and by the same simple action making her very breath temporarily stop and back up within her lungs and throat.

"Because," Alisha finally managed to say, words slowly materializing in a mouth that was bone-dry, "it wouldn't have been genuine. You would have only asked for me so that I wouldn't feel as if I was every patient's second-rate consolation prize. They couldn't get in to see Dan, so they put up with seeing me."

Was that how she really felt about it? Or was she baiting him, seeing how far he'd go to get her to feel confident?

Brett had a feeling it might be a combination of the two.

"Are you a second-rate doctor?" he asked her in a mild, nonjudgmental tone.

"No, of course not," she denied.

Brett heard a little fire in her answer and found it encouraging. She did believe in herself, which was a good thing, but she definitely needed that feeling bolstered.

"Then why the hell would you think that the patients even *think* of you that way?" he quietly demanded.

He would have allowed his voice to become more heated, but he instinctively knew that she guarded her privacy zealously and wanted to keep her conversations that way, as well.

Okay, so they were having an actual serious discussion on the subject, she thought, rather surprised that Brett was capable of being serious. If that was the case, then she might as well level with him.

"Because they all want to see Dan when they come to the clinic," she told Brett.

He shrugged off her reasoning. "It's just easier to go with what you know, with the familiar. There's a sort of unconscious comfort about that—as long as the doctor is competent and doesn't mess up. Give them time, Alisha. The good people of Forever will get used to you, see you for the dedicated doctor that you are."

He'd just called her Alisha, she realized with a sudden inner start. That was the first time he'd used her name instead of calling her Lady Doc.

Had he just done that on purpose? Or was it just a slip of the tongue?

"How would you know I was dedicated?" Alisha challenged.

She wanted him to see that she wasn't going to be taken in by platitudes. If he meant what he said, he was going to have to prove it by convincing her of his reasons.

"For one thing, if you weren't dedicated," Brett said, taking a long drag of his beer, "you wouldn't be out here. And for another, if you weren't good, you wouldn't have all those letters of recommendation to present to Dan at your interview."

Alisha blinked, stunned. The interview had been a private one, conducted between two professionals. "How did you—"

"Small town," Brett reminded her, thinking she really didn't need to be told much more than that to understand what he was saying.

Since he was building his case about her qualifications on her references, she pointed out something she felt was rather obvious. "The letters could have been faked."

How simple-minded did she think the citizens of a small town were? Brett silently marveled, trying not to take offense. Someone like Alisha should have known that brain size had absolutely no real correlation with the town's boundary lines.

"One, Dan's not an idiot. He called some of the doctors whose signatures were on those letters just to make sure everything was legitimate, and two, he's had a chance to observe you in action and he seems to be more than satisfied with you. Dan's not a hard taskmaster, but he's not exactly known as a pushover, either. And he wants the best for his town."

It was growing noisier in the bar again, and Alisha found that she had to raise her voice to be heard, a fact that didn't exactly make her happy.

"Dan told you that?" she asked, torn between being pleased and being less than thrilled that she would be the topic of discussion for the doctor and the bartender, something that sounded like the beginning of a joke recited in a grade-B movie.

"Not exactly," Brett corrected. "Dan told Holly that.

Then she told Ray—her husband," he explained in case Alisha didn't make the connection. "And *Ray* told me when he stopped in for a drink and to catch up. Bottom line, our Dr. Dan is more than satisfied with your efforts, and on top of that, the town's satisfied because they've come to trust Dan's judgment."

It was then that she noticed that Brett had poured her a drink and had eased it in front of her. She gazed down at the glass but refrained from picking it up. "What's this?"

They were back to their customary relationship, and he laughed at her question. "If I have to explain a drink to you, you really do need to get out more, Lady Doc— and to pay attention."

"Yes, I know it's a drink," she replied patiently. "And I know that it's the drink you made for me when we sealed the rental deal for the apartment upstairs. But that doesn't explain why you just made me another one."

Brett's smile was swiftly getting to her. It was almost as if it was actually burrowing under her skin. She explained away the increased heat around her as being the result of the extra bodies that were packed into Murphy's—but if she was being honest with herself, she knew that wasn't really it.

Brett was undoubtedly like that with every woman he served, she reminded herself. The man was a charmer from the word *go,* and she knew all about charmers— they were as shallow as a puddle on a city sidewalk.

"Same reason as the first time," Brett told her easily.

Her eyes narrowed as she looked at the drink, then at him. He hadn't cleared up the situation. "I'm renting another apartment?" she asked drolly.

"No, that drink's yours so we can properly celebrate

your very first patient," he told her. He raised his own glass in a toast—to her. "The first of many who will come through the doors of the clinic, asking for you and seeking out your expertise as well as your delicate touch."

"How would you know if I had a delicate touch or not?" she asked, amused, after she had taken a very long, bracing sip of her drink.

My God, she thought as awareness slipped in. Was she actually flirting with him? Flirting with her landlord? With the bartender? Hadn't she learned her lesson about men like Brett?

She really *was* giddy, wasn't she? Alisha thought in conflicted wonder.

"Now, that's just something I intuitively know," Brett answered, looking down at her hand resting on the bar. He had to tamp down the desire to simply stroke her hand, to run his fingertips over her skin. As he recalled from the all-too-brief contact he'd had with her hand the evening he'd shown her the apartment, it was as smooth as silk to the touch.

"However, if you want to prove me wrong, here I am. Touch me," he invited in a voice that was as seductive as it was gentle.

The look in his eyes was the very definition of *mischievous*—with a very healthy dose of sexiness thrown in to boot.

Had Liam's band just played "Taps"? Or was she hallucinating? Her money, sadly, was on the latter. In either case, she was losing ground, and she knew it.

Chapter Ten

He was daring her. And maybe, just maybe, a part of Brett was laughing at her, as well. Not cruelly—instinct told her that Brett Murphy was not cruel by nature or design—but he was laughing at her in amusement. Amusement that still, no matter how it was sliced, was at her expense.

If only the man didn't look so damn sexy while he was doing it. But even that incensed her, reminding her how vulnerable she'd once been by being attracted to a man's looks.

Now, at least, she knew how to look beneath the veneer.

"Afraid?" Brett asked, his mouth curving.

Her eyes narrowed into small, flashing slits. Brett had inadvertently said just the right thing to galvanize her resolve.

To Alisha, to show fear had always been equal to showing weakness, and to be perceived as weak ripped independence right out of a person's hands. Once lost, independence was incredibly difficult to win back—the same way that trust was difficult to win back once a person was caught in a lie.

She refused to ever be that weak person, and worse, to be perceived as a weak person.

Keeping that thought foremost in her mind, Alisha defiantly placed her hand on top of Brett's, her eyes never leaving his.

"Satisfied?" she fairly bit off.

She watched, her body growing even more heated, as the corners of Brett's firm mouth slowly, seductively, *wickedly* curved upward. She could almost *feel* the impression of his smile within her being. It took her a full second to realize that she'd stopped breathing. Air found its way into her lungs with effort.

"Not by a long shot, Alisha," he whispered, making sure that she was the only one who heard him. Making his response *that* much more intimate.

Alisha.

He'd called her Alisha again. Not the flippant nickname he'd awarded her—Lady Doc—or her title—Dr. Cordell—but her given name. And by using her name the way he did, he made this exchange between them *extremely* intimate despite the fact that there had to be upward of at least fifty-five people milling around the inside of Murphy's.

As if her ability to react was set on some sort of a five-second-delay program, Alisha suddenly pulled back her hand.

"Well, you're going to have to *be* satisfied," she retorted. Pushing her empty glass back toward him on the bar, Alisha rose from the stool. "Thanks for the drink," she told him stiffly.

"My pleasure, darlin'," he said, deliberately incorporating a whimsical Irish brogue into his voice. When she shot him an exasperated look, he winked at her.

He watched as she became flustered, then turned her back to him.

"By the way," he called after her as she started to hurry away, "when's your next day off?"

The question, coming completely out of nowhere, struck her as incredibly odd.

"Why?"

Brett was the picture of nonchalance as he shrugged carelessly. "Thought you might like to get a look at a ranch—or what used to be a ranch," he amended.

Curious, she retraced her steps. Just what was the man up to? "Used to be?" she repeated uncertainly. "What is it now?"

"Deserted," he answered.

He was talking about that property he'd inherited, wasn't he? she suddenly recalled. Exactly what was this charmer's angle? He had to have one because all charmers had an angle.

"You want to take me to a deserted ranch?" she asked incredulously, then came back to the same question she'd already asked. "Why?"

Brett shrugged again as he dried off a section of the bar, his broad shoulders moving like a restless mountain lion surveying the lay of the land before him.

"I thought that maybe you might have some input you'd want to share about the property," he told her. "I'm open to suggestions."

She stared at him. He was kidding, right? "I'm from New York," she reminded him as if that little fact had slipped his mind.

Was she trying to say that since she was a city girl, she had no idea how to view a ranch? "Doesn't mean you can't have a vision, or that you're incapable of ultimately inspiring some good input."

That wasn't why he wanted her to come with him. Alisha looked at him knowingly. "And this has nothing to do with getting me alone on a deserted ranch?" she challenged.

"I'd be lying if I said the thought hadn't crossed my mind," Brett told her, with the appearance of sincerity. "But I'm not looking to put you in a compromising situation," he continued. "And if I do anything to make you pick up and leave, Dan, as well as half the town, will have my head mounted up on a pike as a warning for any other shortsighted Lothario. I just thought you might want to get away from everything for a while, that's all."

Alisha laughed at his flawed reasoning. "Brett, being here in Forever *is* getting away from everything," she emphasized.

"Okay," he allowed, "point taken. *More* away from everything," he amended, this time with a heart-pumping, engaging grin.

Alisha debated back and forth for a few seconds, then told him, "Sunday." With that, she began to walk away from him in earnest.

The noise was once again putting a wall up between them. He knew she'd answered him, but as to what that answer was, he couldn't say for certain. Losing no time, he circumvented the counter, quickly emerging on the other side in order to take a few steps after her and actually *hear* her response.

"What?" he asked, his hand on her shoulder to temporarily stop her in her tracks before she could disappear into the mass of humanity filling up his family's establishment.

Startled, because she hadn't heard him call after her a second time, and she wasn't expecting anyone else to try to get her attention, Alisha attempted to shrug off the masculine hand she felt on her shoulder. She swung around quickly, a confrontational look on her face.

Her features softened the moment she saw who was behind her. "Oh, it's you."

"Me," he agreed, then explained why he'd stopped her. "I didn't hear your answer."

"Sunday," she repeated. "The clinic is closed on Sunday—but I'm on call should anything come up," she deliberately added.

It wasn't just a safety net for her in case she changed her mind about accompanying Brett to this deserted ranch of his; it was also true. When she had become a doctor, she had knowingly agreed to be on call for the rest of her life—or until such time as she was no longer of any useful benefit to the medical community.

For her, becoming a doctor wasn't just a profession; it was also a calling. And, if she was being completely honest, out here she felt there was even more use and need of her skills than in the city where she'd received her training. In New York City, she was a general surgeon. Here, that was still her specialty, but she also got to bandage knees, treat upper respiratory issues and diagnose stomach ailments.

Every day was a challenge the second she crossed the threshold. She had to give 110 percent of herself and apply the same percentage of her skills because she was working in a small town that had no community of physicians for her to fall back on or consult with.

As if reading her mind—the man gave her an eerie feeling that he was capable of doing just that—Brett nodded. "Sure, I understand. If something comes up, that takes precedence. But if there are no medical emergencies, how about I pick you up at nine—or is that too early?" he asked.

Even after being in Forever a month, she was still basically running on New York time, which meant that Brett's nine o'clock was actually more like eleven o'clock for her.

She was accustomed to getting up early and not wasting the morning in bed. "You can make it earlier if you'd like."

She got up early. He liked that. He was an early riser himself. Running Murphy's as well as having had to raise his brothers at one point had trained him to do with a minimum of sleep. His lifestyle encouraged him to get a jump start on each day.

"Eight, then," he said, moving the pickup time up by an hour. Then, with what felt like almost a private smile, he added, "If you change your mind about the time—or about going—you know where to find me."

That Brett had given her an escape clause went a long way in his favor. The next moment, she couldn't help wondering if he was aware of that and had given her a way out for just that purpose.

You're getting way too cynical, 'Lish.

That, too, was due to Pierce, she thought with more than a trace of annoyance. Like the lyric of a song she'd heard on the radio the other morning at Miss Joan's— these people listened to way too much country music, she couldn't help thinking—Pierce had actually *stolen her happy.*

Though she couldn't warm up to country music in general, that lyric, at least, rang very true. Pierce had stolen her happy, her usual sunny way of looking at everything. These days, she weighed everything, took everything apart, searching for the trap, the bad within the good.

She had to do something about that. Otherwise, even though she had broken off her engagement to the philandering surgeon, Pierce had actually won that round—because he had ruined her ability to view things in a positive light when it came to any other man.

And yet, despite everything, there was *something* about Brett...

"So, Sunday at eight is all right?" Brett asked, peering into her face. The look in her eyes told him that at least for a moment, she had gone somewhere far away in her head. He wanted to make sure she hadn't just answered him in the affirmative because she wasn't really listening.

Rousing herself, Alisha said, "It's all right." Then she glanced at his hand, which was still on her shoulder, still anchoring her in place. "Are you planning on releasing my shoulder anytime soon?" she asked, her voice deceptively light.

He hadn't realized that he still had his hand on her shoulder. Probably because he liked making a physical connection with her. He lifted his hand now in a show of compliance.

"Sorry," he told her. Brett took a couple of steps backward, away from her and closer to the bar.

Inclining her head, she silently took his apology and absolved him. The conversation abruptly ended at the same time.

Alisha felt exhausted, just the way she felt every night. The difference being that tonight, along with the exhaustion, there was a host of butterflies, spreading their wings and colliding with each other inside her stomach.

As quickly as she could, she made her way across the crowded room until she finally reached the rear and the staircase. Once there, she paused for a moment, letting out a long breath to steady herself and reclaim her bearings.

She'd agreed to accompany Brett to this so-called property of his. But she could always say no.

At this point, Alisha realized as she took the stairs up to her tiny apartment, she didn't really know if she would go with him on Sunday—or not.

"YOU AND THE lady doc an item?"

The sleepy-sounding question came from Nathan McLane, one of Murphy's steadiest regulars. Married for longer than he could honestly remember, Nathan had for years found his way to the saloon's counter every day after his hours as a clerk at the general store were over.

Now that he was retired, Nathan spent even more time seated at Murphy's, nursing a beer—when he wasn't sleeping off the effects of all those beers in the town's jail.

To the random observer, Nathan appeared to be indifferent to the world around him. But closer scrutiny inevitably showed that the exact opposite was actually true. Nathan absorbed everything that happened around him much the way he absorbed the alcohol in his glass. Slowly and completely, usually without comment.

Brett looked at the man who had occupied that same stool when his uncle Patrick had owned and run Murphy's. Nathan was practically a fixture at the saloon. For a moment, he really thought that he had imagined the regular asking the question.

As much a part of Murphy's as the very bar itself, Nathan at times just seemed to blend into the background despite his unique features. Resembling nothing so much as a sun-bleached haystack tossed atop a rumpled man carrying way too much weight around for his five-ten frame, he was a hard man to take seriously.

But Brett had always accorded Nathan the same amount of respect he gave all his patrons. To that end, he took to heart any question or comment that Nathan made.

"No," Brett replied, wiping down the length of the bar directly in front of Nathan—when he became inebriated, he tended to spill his beer a little. "We're not an item, Nathan. I'm just trying to make her feel like she belongs here. Dr. Dan is working too hard. We need a second doctor in Forever."

A few people along the bar mumbled, adding in their two cents and essentially agreeing with the gist of Brett's statement.

Only Nathan spoke up loud enough for Brett to make out what was being said.

"You could try marrying her," Nathan told him, shifting his gaze to take in the bartender. Bloodshot eyes vainly attempted to focus on the younger man. Giving up, Nathan addressed the rest of his statement to his half-empty beer mug. "Just 'cause it turned out so bad for me doesn't mean it will for you."

A hearty laugh greeted the intoxicated advice. "Are you trying to talk the last of Forever's elite bachelors into giving up his title?" Gabriel Rodriguez asked the question as he came around to stand next to Nathan at the bar. "Of course," Miguel Rodriguez's son continued, making eye contact with Brett, "the last couple of men who boasted that they were never going to tie the knot with any female who walked the earth did just that pretty soon afterward."

It sounded to him as if Gabe was putting him on some sort of notice. He could do that all he wanted, Brett thought. He wasn't going to get married for a *long* time to come.

"You talking about your brothers, Gabe?" Finn asked, coming over to join his brother and Gabe at the far end of the bar.

Although Gabe nodded at Nathan, the latter continued communing with his beer, obviously content to let the conversation go on with his supervision, but not necessarily any of his input.

"Yeah, I am. Didn't really know what I was missing until I got married. None of us did," Gabe said honestly. He put one arm around Nathan's exceedingly wide back, practically straining to do so. "Not everyone follows in old Nathan here's footsteps," he testified. "I sure wouldn't trade what I have now for what I had before for all the money in the world."

He sounded sincere, Brett thought. Most likely, he was. You couldn't fake that sort of *happy*.

"That's because you lucked out," Brett told him. For an instant, he found himself thinking of Laura, the one who had gotten away—or more accurately, the one he had sent away with his refusal to choose between leaving Forever with her and staying in the town with his underage brothers. "Your wife never gave you any ultimatums," he added, saying the last sentence more to himself than to anyone else.

And then he thought of the woman he had just asked to see the ranch with him. "And if you're thinking of Lady Doc," he said, looking at Gabe, knowing how the people in this town were quick to try to pair off singles with likely candidates, "that one still hasn't made up her mind whether or not she's staying in Forever. She might take off for that fancy hospital in New York that she came from."

"If anyone can convince her to stay here, it's you," Gabe replied.

But Brett shook his head. "You're giving me way too much credit here," he told Gabe. "That lady's got a mind all her own, and it's not about to be cajoled or coerced by anything that I or anyone else can say," he assured his friend.

Whatever Gabe might have said to contradict Brett's statement never managed to be uttered because another, more pressing matter suddenly took front and center for not just him or Brett, but for just about everyone who was in the saloon.

Nathan had made a strange gurgling sound as he clutched his right side. He attempted to say something to Brett, but nothing coherent came out. The next moment, still clutching his side, Nathan made a guttural sound. His eyes rolled back in his head and then he fell off his bar stool with a resounding thud.

Chapter Eleven

"Is he dead?" a high-pitched voice in the center of the crowd asked as the man the voice belonged to tried to jockey for a better position.

"Naw, probably just dead drunk," the man next to him answered with a dismissive laugh.

A tight knot of people had formed around the heavy-set, unconscious man on the floor, and the participants all seemed to be intent on coming in even closer, despite the lack of space.

The second Nathan keeled over, Brett quickly made his way out from behind the bar. Finn was directly behind him. Moving people aside, Brett reached Nathan's prone body.

Gabe was already crouching on the floor beside the man, feeling for Nathan's pulse. It was obvious by the expression on Gabe's face that he hadn't succeeded in locating it yet. "I can't find his pulse, Brett."

"Ah, don't worry. McLane's pulse is probably just buried under all that fat," another patron volunteered, slurring some of his words a little.

Brett, always more than ready to share a joke, appeared to be deadly serious as he shouted out instructions. "Finn, keep these mindless comedians back.

Nathan needs space. Gabe, you keep trying to rouse Nathan."

"Where are you going?" Finn asked as Brett pushed his way out of the inner circle of curious onlookers.

"To get our own private doctor," Brett tossed over his shoulder, hurrying to the rear of the saloon.

Once there, Brett took the stairs two at a time, reaching Alisha's door in record time. Rather than knocking on it lightly, a sense of urgency had Brett doubling up his fist and pounding. He hadn't liked the way Nathan had looked, and he knew enough about medicine to know that sometimes, every second counted. This might very well be one of those times.

On the other side of the door, Alisha had just finished changing out of the clothes that she'd worn all day and into a baggy T-shirt that had seen far better days and a pair of denim shorts that had long since faded to a shade of nondescript blue. Ready for a quiet hour or two before bedtime, she was startled by the pounding on her door.

Had one of the men downstairs had too much to drink and decided that what he really wanted was some female companionship? They'd looked like a harmless bunch when she'd walked past them, but looks could be deceiving, and it was better to be safe than sorry.

Alisha glanced around for something to drag over to her door to keep whoever was pounding from breaking in. The only thing that presented itself was one of the two chairs at her small table. It was flimsy, but it was all she had.

She was about to grab it when she thought she heard Brett's voice calling to her.

"Are you in there, Doc? I've got a man down, and I need you to look at him for me."

Alisha stared at the door uncertainly, her nerves on edge. Was Brett serious? Or was that just a ploy to get into her room?

"Alisha, please. I don't know if he's breathing."

That did it for her. Alisha flipped the lock and pulled open her door.

Brett appeared worried and far more serious than she had ever seen him.

"What happened?" she asked.

"I'll tell you downstairs," he promised, already heading back to the stairs. But when he turned to look over his shoulder, he saw that Alisha wasn't following behind him. "Doc?" he called out, confused. "Where'd you go?"

The next moment, Alisha came hurrying over to him, her medical bag in tow. "Had to get my bag," she explained.

This almost felt like a stereotypical scenario, she couldn't help thinking. Here she was, dashing down the stairs in the shank of the night, clutching her medical bag, ready to minister to some unfortunate soul who'd been on the wrong end of a bar fight or had tripped and smashed his head.

Or—

At that point, it suddenly occurred to Alisha that she didn't have a clue exactly what was waiting for her.

The noise level was drowning out almost everything else by now. She raised her voice so that Brett could hear her. "What happened?" she cried.

Brett turned his head so that his voice would carry toward her. "Damned if I know. One minute, Nathan is sitting on his usual stool, drinking beer like he does every night. The next, he clutches his side, makes a funny whimpering noise and falls on the floor."

"His side, not his chest?" she asked. The first thing she'd thought of was a heart attack.

At her side now, Brett shook his head. "No, it was definitely his side."

"Which?" she asked as they came into the saloon proper. "Right or left?" She was fairly shouting now.

"His right, I think." Rethinking the incident, Brett confirmed his first answer. "It was definitely his right."

It seemed as if everyone in the saloon had gathered around the fallen man, forming a very large, almost impenetrable ring around Nathan, even with Finn trying to hold the patrons back.

Brett moved protectively in front of the woman he'd gone to fetch and, pushing the throng aside, created a path for Alisha.

"Get back," he ordered. "Everyone, get back. Give the doc some room." It wasn't a request voiced in his usual easygoing manner. This was a command, issued in a no-nonsense tone of voice.

The people in the crowd obediently parted and began to move to either side of the immobile form sprawled on his side on the floor.

Gabe rose to his feet to get out of Alisha's way. "Want us to move him for you?" he asked.

"Not until I know what we're up against," she responded.

Taking out her stethoscope, she sank down to her knees. Putting both ends into her ears, she listened intently as she moved the stethoscope around the man's wide chest. The effort quickly met with success. She could make out the beat of his heart.

The beat was elevated.

Placing her hand to the man's forehead—not the last word in medicine, she knew, but useful just the same—told her that Nathan's temperature was raised, as well.

Not good.

Removing the stethoscope from her ears for a moment, she looked up at Brett. "Could you turn Mr. McLane on his back, please?"

"Finn?" Brett said to his brother, his meaning clear. This effort was going to take two of them.

Brett and his brother moved Nathan so that the unconscious man was flat on the floor, then moved back, out of the doctor's way.

Very gingerly, Alisha passed her small hands slowly and methodically along Nathan's lower right quadrant. She watched his face as she did so. Despite the fact that he was still unconscious, she saw the man wince and heard him cry out in obvious pain. Loudly.

When he did, several of Murphy's patrons, who were angling for a closer position to get a better look at what was going on, jumped back, clearly shaken. The next second, they appeared to be embarrassed because they'd reacted like children around a campfire, listening to ghost stories and jumping when they heard a noise behind them.

The resulting cacophony of explanations and excuses proved to be only just so much more incomprehensible background noise to Alisha.

Unable to hold his curiosity in check any longer, Gabe asked her, "What's the matter with him, Doc? Is he going to make it?"

Brett seconded that concern. "Is he going to be all right?" he asked.

She didn't like to make prognoses until she had all the facts—or as many as were available in a situation. "I can't tell until I open him up—"

Her reply immediately caused a stir amid the bar's clients. She could have sworn she heard someone laying odds on the outcome.

"You're going to operate on him here?" Finn exclaimed in obvious awe and wonder. "Wow!"

"No, not here," she immediately corrected, then turned to look up at Brett. "We need to get Nathan to the clinic," she told him. "No offense, but your floor isn't exactly sterile."

"Yeah, but neither's Brett," someone in the crowd called out, laughing and obviously amusing himself.

Brett ignored the mindless remark as well as the man who'd uttered it. His only concern right now was Nathan. "What's wrong with him?" he asked Alisha pointedly.

She was about to repeat her previous vague comment, but the genuine concern she saw in Brett's eyes had her reconsidering. Instead of saying it was too early to tell, she reviewed the symptoms and gave the man her best guess.

"He's running a fever, he clutched his side when he collapsed and his side is swollen and so tender, he can't bear to be touched even in his unconscious state. It looks pretty much like appendicitis to me." And, she added silently, she was more than 95 percent certain that she was right.

"Can't be that. Nathan had his appendix removed when he was a kid," one of the female patrons volunteered as she made her way to the front of the human circle.

"Sometimes they grow back," Alisha answered. "It's rare, but it is possible. Like I said, I won't know exactly what we're up against until I open him up." Accepting the hand Brett extended to her, she stood. The way she saw it, her immediate problem was one of leverage—and transport. "I'm going to need help getting Nathan to the clinic." That made her think of something else. "And I also need someone to get the doctor."

Finn looked at her, confused. "But *you're* the doctor."

Alisha smiled at that. It looked as though she was finally being accepted here, and not just by one lone female patient.

Still, she wasn't vain enough to think she could do this on her own—unless she absolutely had to. And right now, she didn't. She was perfectly happy just assisting at the surgery, since she surmised that Dan would want to be the primary surgeon.

Nathan was drastically overweight, which meant that there would be abundant layers of tissue and fat to cut through before she could even get at the appendix and remove it. That was better left to a man with experience with this sort of thing.

"The *other* doctor," she stressed. "Dr. Davenport."

"I'll do it," Finn volunteered.

"Okay," Gabe said, coming to stand beside Brett. They both looked down at the moaning, unconscious man on the floor. "That leaves us with the problem of getting Nathan over to the clinic."

"If we had a gurney, we could just wheel him over," Alisha said, thinking out loud. "Except that we don't."

Purchasing a gurney was on her wish list. If she was

going to remain here for any amount of time, it might as well be under better conditions. Or at least the very best conditions she was able to create.

"We can drive him over in my flatbed truck," Gabe offered. "We just have to get him in the back."

Just.

The single word hung in the air, mocking her as she tried to come up with a viable solution that would get her patient into the back of the flatbed without doing him any harm.

"Problem is," she told Gabe and Brett, "if it *is* his appendix, it might be on the verge of rupturing, and if we jostle him too much when we try to get him into the truck, it might just burst."

"In other words, you don't want us to each grab a limb and carry him outside," Brett said, interpreting her words. In a pinch, that would have been what he would have done—get three other men and between them, carry Nathan to the back of the truck that way.

"That wouldn't be wise," she said seriously, trying to think of an alternative. And then a possible solution occurred to her. "If we can get Nathan onto a big blanket and each grabbed a corner of *that,* we might be able to get away with it. That's a little more cushioned than just dragging him by his arms and legs." She turned to Brett. "Do you have a big blanket?"

"Technically, *you* do," he told her. When she looked at him, waiting for an explanation, he said, "There's a folded-up blanket on the top shelf in your closet. For cold winter nights," he added.

"Can you go get it, please?" she requested.

Brett was already hurrying toward the stairs again. "On my way."

Waiting, Alisha bent down and placed her fingers against Nathan's forehead again. It was even hotter than it had been before.

Not a good sign, she thought in frustration.

"Does Nathan have any family?" she asked Gabe as she rose to her feet again.

"He's got a wife," Gabe told her.

It was always good to cover all bases. If her husband was sick, she'd definitely want to be notified. "Maybe someone should go get her," she suggested, looking around the saloon for a volunteer.

"Hell, Henrietta's not going to like having to come down here on account of Nathan," one of the men standing behind her said. There was a murmur of agreement.

"Even if he's really sick?" Alisha asked in disbelief.

"Henrietta'll only say that it serves him right, coming here night after night instead of home to her," another man spoke up, agreeing with his friend.

That just didn't seem right to her.

Ordinarily, she would have just shrugged the matter off. Dealing with all sorts of people in New York had made her somewhat removed from this kind of personal drama. But things were different out here, and she had come to expect a certain level of compassionate behavior from the citizens of Forever.

Consequently, Nathan's wife's behavior seemed horribly insensitive to her. Without fully realizing it, she wasn't going to just stand on the sidelines and let that type of behavior continue. Not when this man needed someone in his corner.

Turning around to face the last man who had spoken up about Nathan's wife, she ordered, "You go and tell that woman to get her butt in gear and bring it over to the clinic. If I'm going to try to save her husband's life, she needs to be there for her man."

Stunned for a moment, the man's thin lips peeled back to display a toothy grin. It was obvious that he liked what he'd heard.

"You got it, Doc," he told her with enthusiasm— and then took off, intent on following her instructions.

Brett reappeared with a blanket in tow and had returned just in time to hear Alisha issue her order in no uncertain terms, dispatching Warren Tate to go get Nathan's wife. There was no question about it. He liked what he had heard.

He grinned, offering the blanket to Alisha. "You can be pretty tough when you want to be," he said. The admiration in his voice would have been impossible to miss.

"Must be all this clean air I've been breathing. Goes straight to my head," she quipped drily.

After shaking out the blanket, Alisha proceeded to spread it out on the floor right next to Nathan's very large form.

She straightened out one end and stepped back. "Okay, I need four very strong men to each grab a limb and, as gently as possible, place Mr. McLane onto that blanket. Then we have to carry him very gingerly to the street and load him onto Gabe's flatbed."

This was *so* not going to be easy, she thought, even as she said the words. The plan sounded simple enough to execute, but her unexpected patient was beyond huge, and they were dealing with a medical emergency that was on the delicate side. If Nathan's appendix ruptured during the transport, she would have only a limited amount of time to clean out the area and keep Nathan from succumbing to peritonitis.

Definitely not ideal conditions.

Crossing her fingers both literally and mentally, Alisha moved completely out of the way and allowed Brett, Gabe and two other men, both huskier than the first two, to lift Nathan and place him as gently as humanly possible onto the blanket.

With Brett taking charge, the four men moved in concert and practically in slow motion. Though unconscious, Nathan still cried out in pain when they finally set him down on the blanket.

The noise shot right through her.

Alisha could have sworn she actually *felt* Nathan McLane's pain.

There was such a thing as being too in sync with her patient.

The silent lecture didn't help. Her empathy continued flowing until her supply of the emotion was all but gone.

When the men each picked up a corner of the blanket, Alisha felt an overwhelming desire to join in and take a corner or a section of blanket herself. She wanted to join the effort to help get Nathan into the flatbed, but she knew that rather than help, she'd undoubtedly just be in the way.

So she held her breath and followed at a decent distance away, watching as Brett gave out orders, reminding everyone to exercise extreme caution when they carefully got the big man into the back of Gabe's truck.

He was a leader, she thought in silent admiration—and, inexplicably, with pride. He wasn't the kind of man who hung back. He only gave that impression at the bar because it suited him.

Gabe drove his flatbed to the clinic.

To her surprise, Brett presented himself at the driver's side of her car just as she was about to get in herself. "I'll drive you to the clinic if you're too tired," he offered.

The offer had that strange, warm feeling materializing again, the one that only he seemed capable of re-creating for her.

This wasn't the time, she told herself. She had a patient—possibly a life to save.

"No, I'm fine, thanks."

Adrenaline had taken care of her fatigue, immediately kicking in the moment she saw Nathan on the floor. She suspected, as she put her key into the ignition, that she was going to be running on adrenaline for a good long time.

When Brett rounded the front hood of her car and slid into the shotgun seat beside her, she was certain of it.

"You didn't think I wasn't going to come along, did you?" he asked. "Nathan's a longtime customer—and a friend. Sometimes, it feels like I'm his only friend," he added. "I'm not leaving him alone at a time like this."

"You don't think his wife's going to come?" she asked, starting the car.

"I'm not a betting man," Brett told her. "But if I were..." For a second, his voice trailed off, and then he said, "The odds are less than fifty-fifty that she'll come."

She'd never met the woman, but Alisha decided that she didn't like Henrietta McLane.

And she was finding reasons—even though she wasn't looking for them—to like Brett Murphy more and more.

Chapter Twelve

Parking at an angle in front of the clinic, Alisha quickly jumped out of her vehicle less than ten minutes later.

"Hold up!" she shouted to Gabe. The latter was already out of the cab of his truck and on his way to the back of the flatbed. The men appeared ready to carry Nathan into the darkened clinic.

"Why?" Gabe called back to her.

Alisha didn't waste time with an explanation. Instead, she turned toward Brett and instructed, "Make sure he doesn't move Nathan."

Confused, Brett looked over to the flatbed, where Nathan lay, unconscious, on the blanket. "You're not planning on operating out here, are you?" he asked her incredulously. "Hell, my saloon's cleaner than his flatbed."

But Alisha wasn't heading back to the truck; she was going in the opposite direction. "Just wait," she shouted over her shoulder as she unlocked the door and disappeared into the clinic.

Brett stood where he was, wondering what she was up to. He watched as first one light, then another went on in the clinic, marking her progress through the building. Since there'd been no light in the building when they'd arrived, he assumed that Finn hadn't gotten back with Dan yet and wondered what the holdup was. The fact that Warren Tate, the man Alisha had dispatched to bring Nathan's wife, hadn't returned with the woman was far less of a surprise. Henrietta McLane was not a woman to be coerced into doing anything she didn't want to do.

The next minute, he forgot about Finn and Dan as well as whether anyone could manage to get Nathan's wife to show any concern for her husband. Alisha had returned, and she was pushing the clinic's one hospital bed in front of her. The bed was used primarily for patients who needed to remain under observation overnight at the clinic.

Brett was quick to join her. "Here, let me," he said, taking over. It was obvious to him that she was having some difficulty getting the bed to go where she wanted it to, despite the fact that it had wheels.

Alisha gladly stepped back. "It's not a gurney," she explained, "but at least it's mobile, and I figured it would be easier getting Nathan in on this than trying to carry him in on the blanket."

Brett grinned as he maneuvered the bed until it was parallel to the flatbed opening. "Hell of a lot better than risking dropping Nathan on the ground," he agreed. The others looked relieved not to have to carry the big man into the building.

It was still a tricky proposition, lifting and carrying Nathan from the back of the flatbed onto the hospital bed. Even with the blanket beneath the man and the fact that there were four of them doing the maneuvering, it was still by no means an easy transfer. All four were gasping for air by the time they got the man onto the bed.

Alisha released the breath she'd been holding during the short, taxing ordeal. "Get him into the last exam room."

She was grateful that Liam had elected to come along with them. The youngest of the brothers had walked into Murphy's just in time to see Brett, Gabe and two other men struggling to get Nathan into the flatbed. Wanting to help, he'd gotten into Gabe's truck.

Brett paused for a second before following Alisha's request. Turning toward Liam, he decided that his youngest brother, with his boyish appeal, might just be able to succeed where the previous man sent on the errand had failed. "Why don't you go and see if you can get Mrs. McLane to come here. Lady Doc sent Warren Tate to get her, but he obviously didn't have any luck."

Liam seemed torn for a moment between doing what his older brother asked and wanting to see what happened next. But in the end, he nodded.

"Sure," he agreed. "I'll bring her back." It didn't seem to occur to Liam as he hurried out that Nathan's wife would refuse to come. Liam, Brett knew, still believed that when push came to shove, people always did the right thing, and he approached everything he did in that light.

Let's hope you're right, Liam, Brett thought, getting back to the job at hand.

When Brett and Gabe finally pushed the hospital bed back into the last exam room, he saw that Alisha was already there. She'd donned blue scrubs over her T-shirt and jean shorts and was busy scrubbing her hands.

"Blue's a nice color on you," Brett noted wryly.

"It'll be an even nicer color when Dr. Davenport gets here," she told him. Dan didn't live that far from the clinic; he should have been here by now, she thought. "What do you think is keeping him?"

Brett's shoulders rose and fell in a vague shrug. "Your guess is as good as mine," he replied. "Maybe he thinks that now that you're here, he can ease up a little bit, not hurry as much."

She supposed there was a validity to Brett's thinking, but she wasn't altogether sure if that reasoning really fit the man she'd come to know these past few weeks. He seemed far too dedicated to her to be blasé when one of his patients needed him.

"Still doesn't explain why he's not here," she replied. "He's the most dedicated physician I've ever met."

"I can go see what the holdup is," Gabe volunteered.

Alisha flashed a grateful smile at the rancher. "Would you?"

Gabe was already on his way out. "Sure thing."

As Gabe crossed the threshold, Nathan groaned loudly, seeming to rouse himself. His eyelids fluttered as if he was trying to struggle back to consciousness and having a really hard time of it.

"Where—where am I?" Nathan moaned, slurring his words.

About to dry her hands, Alisha was at her patient's side in a heartbeat. "Mr. McLane, it's Dr. Cordell. Are you in much pain?" she asked, bending over the man so that they could make eye contact.

Nathan attempted to take in a breath and groaned even louder. "It feels…like someone's…ripping…open my…gut with a…rusty can opener!" he cried.

Brett was right beside her, ready to help any way he

could. "I think you can take that as a yes," he told her. There was concern in his eyes as he asked, "Do you think you're going to be able to do what's necessary if Dan doesn't show up?"

Squaring her shoulders as if mentally preparing herself for that eventuality, she answered, "I guess I'll have to." She'd operated before, but not since she'd arrived in Forever and never on a man this size. Nathan's girth presented a unique set of circumstances that added to the seriousness of the operation. The nearest full-service hospital was an hour away.

Bending over Nathan again, she told the man in a calm, soft voice, "It's going to be all right, Nathan. We're going to make you better."

Nathan was clutching the sides of the bed, his knuckles all but white as he twisted in pain. "Just shoot me."

"Can't do that, Nathan. It's against the doctor code," Alisha quipped to cover the nervousness she felt right now. Where *was* the doctor? "I'm only allowed to shoot patients as a very last resort—and then only at the end of the month." She heard the clinic door open and close again, and she exhaled a huge sigh of relief. "Oh, thank God. Dan's here," she declared happily to her patient.

The next moment, as she took one look at Dan when he walked in, her obvious relief turned to confusion and real concern.

"What happened to you?" she cried in palpable distress.

Dan had walked in ahead of Finn. The first thing the other people in the room noticed was the fact that the doctor's right arm was immobilized in a sling.

Forever's first resident physician in thirty years appeared almost sheepish as he answered her question.

"I tripped on a tree root and put my hand out to break my fall—which, as it turned out, was the wrong thing to do in this case."

Alisha glared at the man she'd been counting on to take over in stricken horror. "You broke your arm?" she cried, appalled.

Dan shook his head. "Not exactly. I tore my rotator cuff. Problem is, right now it hurts like hell just to move my hand," he told her. "I'm going to have Tina drive me to the hospital in Pine Ridge tomorrow so I can have this thing x-rayed. Maybe I didn't tear any muscles. Maybe it just feels that way," he said hopefully.

But even as Dan said that to her, they both knew he was just trying to deny the obvious.

There was only one thing that mattered right now. "This means you can't operate," Alisha concluded. She could almost feel the lead weight on her chest.

"Can't hold a scalpel, I take it?" Brett asked the man.

Dan's frustration was evident in his eyes. "Can't even wiggle my fingers right now. Don't worry," he told Alisha when he saw the disheartened look on her face. "It'll get better."

She had no doubt that it would—but that didn't do either of them any good right now. "Not in time to save Nathan," she replied.

Dan made his way to the hospital bed, which was now positioned in the center of the room so that Nathan was accessible from any point. "Finn told me that you think it's appendicitis."

Alisha inclined her head. "That's the most logical conclusion, but we won't know until you open him up. I mean—"

"You're going to have to be the one to open him up," Dan said matter-of-factly. Turning from Nathan, who had once again lapsed into unconsciousness from the sheer pain he was experiencing, Dan faced his new associate. "Ever perform an appendectomy before?"

"Yes, but in a hospital with staff, and this person is particularly…large," she finally said for lack of a better term.

"Don't worry," he told her, sounding extremely confident in her estimation. "You'll do fine. I'll talk you through it." Dan looked around the room. "Holly's not here?"

"I didn't think to get her," Alisha confessed. Her main focus, other than getting Nathan to the clinic, had been getting Dan to take over. Now that wasn't going to happen.

"I can call her for you," Gabe volunteered.

But Dan had taken a closer look at the patient and he now shook his head. "No time." He eyed the two men and then made his choice. "Looks like you're going to have to play nurse, Brett."

Rather than balk at the suggestion, Brett nodded. His life had prepared him for stepping up whenever the occasion demanded it. "Sure. Whatever you need."

"Scrub in, Brett." Dan pointed toward the small sink on the far side of the wall. "You're going to be handing Alisha her instruments."

Brett was game to do whatever they needed him to do. "As long as you point them out," he qualified, "since I can't tell one thing from another."

"No problem," Dan assured him with a smile. "Luckily, I didn't tear anything in my mouth."

IN THE END, the surgery wound up taking longer than any of them had expected.

The operation itself had been going along well—until Alisha, after cutting through the layers of skin, tissue and fat, just barely touched Nathan's swollen appendix with the tip of her scalpel. The small organ immediately ruptured, sending toxic fluid throughout Nathan's abdominal cavity.

Alisha had to go into double time, frantically mopping up the mess inside her patient as quickly as she could in an attempt to contain the infection to the best of her ability.

A one-hour simple procedure, encumbered by Nathan's girth and the state of his appendix, wound up turning into an operation that took upward of two and a half hours to complete.

All of her efforts proved fruitful. The end result was that Nathan had survived and gave every sign of being on the road to recovery. Even so, Dan made a judgment call and decided that the man needed to remain in the clinic overnight.

"Why don't you go home?" he suggested to Alisha as they sat in a room away from where Nathan was recovering. "You've more than proven yourself tonight. My contribution will be to stay and watch over him."

As tempting as that was, she knew she couldn't take Dan up on it. "Because you need your rest," she told the man. "You're going to Pine Ridge in the morning to get that shoulder of yours x-rayed, remember?"

Dan tried to shrug off her words, but the action cost him dearly.

"It can wait," he told her, wincing with pain.

"No," Alisha insisted, "it can't." Hands on her hips,

she leveled a glare at the other doctor. "We're not having this argument, Doctor. The town needs you, and you need to have your shoulder fixed up. You're going home. I'm staying. End of discussion," she declared with finality.

Dan shook his head. It was obvious he was amused at her feistiness.

"You are one very stubborn woman," he told her.

If he thought he was going to flatter her into going along with him, he was in for a surprise. "You have no idea," she warned Dan.

"I'd do as she says if I were you, Dan. And don't worry about her," Brett told his friend. "I'll stick around until morning to make sure everything's all right—with her and with Nathan."

Alisha noted that Dan took the other man at his word and that Brett's taking over the way he proposed all seemed perfectly natural to the other doctor. There was obviously a lot of trust going around, and she found that both unusual—so different from the atmosphere she'd just come from—and incredibly heartening, as well.

"If you're sure," Dan said, already backing out of the room.

"You really don't have to stay here," she told Brett once Dan was out of the room and out of earshot. "I know you said what you did to put Dan's mind at ease, but you really don't have to play babysitter here. I can handle the situation."

"Nobody said you couldn't, but maybe I want to stay," Brett said, surprising her. "Did you stop to consider that?"

She couldn't tell if he was actually serious or just pulling her leg. His expression was entirely unreadable. She still gave him the only answer she could in this case. "No."

"Well, consider it. Because I do," he assured her firmly.

This was a man who thrived in the organized chaos that throbbed through his establishment, Alisha thought. His wanting to remain here with her like this made no sense.

"Why would you want to stay here?" she asked, wanting to understand his reasoning—if that was possible. "It's quiet."

His smile was slow and sexy as it slipped across his lips. "Lady Doc, you might have just answered your own question."

She eyed Brett uncertainly. "You *like* the quiet?"

The smile widened a fraction. "Always have."

Okay, he was messing with her, she decided. He *had* to be. "But you run Murphy's. During work hours, that place is as noisy as the middle of Grand Central station."

"Which is why the quiet is appealing to me," Brett countered.

She was too tired to continue with this and just shook her head, surrendering. "You are a complicated man, Brett Murphy."

The sexy smile softened around the edges as he told her, "Right back at you, Lady Doc."

Exhausted, with her thoughts colliding into one another in her head, she blinked. "You think I'm a complicated man?"

Brett laughed. "No, just complicated. I'm not that simple. I do know the difference between a man and a woman," he assured her with a wink that went straight to her stomach and bored a hole there, making itself right at home.

Alisha laughed then, or maybe it was the exhaustion, stretched to another level and making her giddy. "I'm sure you do."

Brett studied her for a moment, his eyes moving along her so slowly, she could have *sworn* she felt them touching her.

"What's that supposed to mean?" he finally asked good-naturedly.

A sigh escaped her lips as she searched for the right words, words that kept eluding her right now. "Just that you were probably born flirting. Born making women weak in the knees," she added.

His eyes were caressing her, undoing her, she thought nervously, unable to look away.

"How about you, Lady Doc?" he asked in a quiet voice. "Do I make your knees weak?"

She tried to brazen it out, although she knew that she was doomed to failure. "I'm sitting down. My knees are fine."

Brett pretended to give her a long once-over, going from her head to her toes. She had discarded the scrubs and was back to wearing only her shorts and T-shirt. He couldn't help wondering if she knew just how enticing she was in that simple little outfit.

She was a woman who wasn't even aware of her sexuality—which made her all the more sexy to the casual observer.

"Yes, they are, just like the rest of you," he told her.

She laughed softly to herself as she shook her head. "There you go again, flirting."

Instead of denying it, or saying something flippant

in his defense, Brett smiled into her eyes. "How'm I doing?" he asked her, his voice low, stirring, as it seemed to slowly, seductively undulate beneath and along her skin.

Alisha was finding that she was definitely having difficulty breathing. The very way this man was looking at her with his deep green eyes seemed to completely paralyze her.

It took effort for her to finally whisper an answer to his question. "Like someone should pass a law against you."

His eyes still holding hers prisoner, he cocked his head in amusement and asked, "I'm that bad?"

Damn but she wished he'd stop whispering like that and speak up. His whispering was making her blood rush through her veins like a stock car crossing the finish line in the Indy 500.

"No," Alisha finally replied with some effort. "You're that good."

Brett was skimming his fingertips along her face, as if he was attempting to memorize every single feature through them.

"Can't have that," he told her.

The next moment, as his eyes continued to hold hers captive, Brett began to lower his mouth to hers in what felt like slow motion.

It felt as if hours had passed before he finally kissed her.

And made time stop completely.

There was surprise on her part.

Surprise and then pleasure.

Surprise that it had happened at all after her silent promises about never allowing herself to be in a compromising situation again. Pleasure because, well, that was really self-explanatory. His kiss was sheer pleasure. And she couldn't resist it—not even a little.

Alisha gave herself permission, just for this single moment in time, to enjoy what was happening and to kiss this man back. Five minutes from now—if not sooner—she would return to being herself, to being vigilantly on her guard.

But for now, for the next three hundred seconds, she wanted just to feel desirable again. Or at least pretend that she was. And most of all, she wanted to celebrate because she had saved a life. Not assisted in saving a life, but had actually been the instrumental person in saving that life. And that felt absolutely wonderful.

As did being kissed by Brett Murphy.

Chapter Thirteen

You're taking advantage of her.

Brett could almost *hear* the voice in his head taking him to task for what he was doing. For what he was so obviously enjoying.

The voice—his conscience, he supposed—was coming in loud and clear.

He'd also realized at that exact moment that he'd wanted to do this, wanted to kiss this rare woman who had come into their midst, from the very first time he had laid eyes on her.

Granted, Alisha hadn't exactly looked friendly when Dan had initially brought her around, but that didn't matter. The connection he had felt when their eyes first met was on a whole different level than what he figured even she was aware of. For him, it was a little like flipping through a magazine and having his attention suddenly seized by a photograph of a top model. Being so captivated by the woman that he promised himself that, someday, he was going to meet that woman and have a relationship with her, no matter how far-fetched that might have seemed.

For Brett, someday had arrived.

The woman who had returned his kiss was *not* the

doctor who ministered to the patients who came to the clinic seeking help. That woman was professional, skilled and dedicated. This woman, the one he was kissing, was a barely bridled wildcat. He could literally taste it in her kiss.

WHAT IS GOING ON with me? Alisha's brain all but screamed at her.

Have you lost your mind? she upbraided herself.

What in heaven's name was she doing, kissing Brett? He was her landlord, for heaven's sake, and granted, the man *was* sexy as all hell, but she'd promised herself never to let something like that, something so shallow as looks, sway her.

Okay, he seemed kinder and deeper than Pierce had been, but the bottom line remained: Brett was an extremely good-looking man, and good-looking men were true only to themselves and their needs. Hadn't she already experienced that firsthand? How many times did it take for the lesson to be driven home for her? Did she really *need* to go through the anguish of a refresher course where all her plans instantly turned to burned dust?

C'mon, Alisha. You've got more self-control than that, don't you?

Trying to keep her arguments for *why* this couldn't be happening uppermost in her mind, Alisha drew her head back, breaking the delicious contact. Just as she did, she felt Brett drawing away, as well, as if her pulling away could be construed as a time-out.

Or maybe the man had satisfied whatever urge had prompted him to kiss her in the first place.

Whichever way it went down, she was going to find a way to use this to her advantage, Alisha silently promised herself. Popping up to her feet while ignoring the hand that he offered her, she quickly strode to the back of the clinic to look in on her patient.

Recovering from the operation, Nathan was still asleep. Even though she wasn't expecting any surprises at this point, someone, Alisha felt, should remain with the man, and since she'd told Dan to go home, she figured that she was the logical choice.

But when she walked into the room where she had performed the operation, she was surprised to find Dan sitting in a chair by the hospital bed. He looked up when she walked in.

Stunned, she stared at the other doctor. "I thought you went home."

"I changed my mind," he informed her in his quiet, authoritative voice.

"But—" She got no further than that.

"You did a great job, Alisha," he told her. "Now I want you to do me a favor and go home and get some rest. You've earned it."

Didn't anyone in this town listen to reason? she wondered. "You can't stay here with Nathan," she insisted. "You're injured."

From his countenance, Alisha could tell she wasn't going to win this debate. Dan had obviously dug in— and he was the senior doctor here. "My shoulder is injured. The rest of me is doing just fine. Now go," he urged.

"But—"

"That part's fine, too," Dan assured her with as straight a face as he could maintain, under the circumstances.

Just then, Brett came in, drawn by the voices and

wondering if Nathan had woken up. In which case, he thought Alisha might need a helping hand with the man.

"You're back," Brett said to Dan in surprise.

"Never actually left," Dan corrected his friend. He turned toward Brett to enlist his assistance. "Do me a favor, Brett. Get our heroic doctor here back to her place. It seems that she won't leave without an armed escort."

Brett was more than willing to comply. "I'm not armed, but I will escort."

Well, she couldn't make the other doctor leave, but by the same token, he couldn't force her to go, either. Of the three of them, she decided, Brett had the least reason to stay.

"You can go home," she urged Brett.

"And so can you," both Brett and Dan chorused together as if they had been practicing delivering that one line for a long time instead of saying it spontaneously.

Alisha opened her mouth, then shut it again. She couldn't fight both of them, and she knew it. Besides, she really *was* tired. Thinking the matter over, she decided that she was going to need both her sleep *and* her strength tomorrow since Dan was going to Pine Ridge to get that shoulder of his x-rayed. That meant that she would be the only doctor on call at the clinic the whole day.

The very thought of that was exhausting right now.

"Okay," she said, reluctantly giving in. "I'll go," she told Dan, but added a condition to her capitulation. "But only if you promise to call me the second you're feeling weak or tired."

Dan nodded. "Already have you on speed dial," he

told her, holding up the cell phone Tina had gotten him for his last birthday.

Sure he did, Alisha thought, looking at the phone skeptically. Still, she didn't feel up to challenging him and, instead, reminded him that "I can be here in five minutes flat."

Now, there was something she couldn't have ever said in New York, Alisha thought. Not with the way that traffic clogged the streets even in the dead of night. Here she could boast being able to make that sort of time in the middle of the day—as well as all the hours in between.

Dan nodded, not that he had the least inclination to summon her—unless the clinic caught on fire. "Good to know," he said mildly, then turned toward Brett. "Get this woman out of here before she falls asleep on her feet, Brett," he ordered.

"You got it." Brett slipped his hand through his tenant's arm and very gently steered her toward the front of the clinic as well as the front door.

They had almost reached it when there was a commotion on the other side of it. The door had been left unlocked, and the person causing the racket pushed it open and marched right into the clinic, still being loud—and practically breathing fire.

Alisha stopped walking and stared at the large, heavyset woman with the round, angry face. This was the way trouble would look if trouble could take a human form.

"Where is he? Where's that lazy, good-for-nothing faker of a husband of mine?" Henrietta McLane demanded as she took the hallway in less than half the strides that Alisha had made on her initial entrance. Glaring at her, the woman snapped, "Is he back there?"

Accosting her, the woman pointed toward the rear of the clinic. More than twice as large as Alisha and a good foot taller, Henrietta McLane was a force to be reckoned with, and not in a good way. Years ago, her girth accustomed her to ignoring others and always getting her own way.

About to intervene, Brett watched in surprise as Alisha got in front of Nathan's charging wife, physically putting her body in the way to stop the woman from going to the back.

"I'm afraid you can't go in there. Mr. McLane is asleep now," Alisha told the woman.

Henrietta snorted, dismissing the access denial and the woman who had delivered it. "He always sleeps off a drunk, missy—nothing new there. I don't know what's gotten into him, but that man has to know that he can't yank me around like this." Saying that, Nathan's wife began to go around Alisha.

For a second time, Alisha deliberately put herself in the larger woman's path.

As she glared at the woman, Henrietta's complexion began to turn a bright shade of red.

"He's not yanking you around," Alisha told her calmly. Maybe the woman was angry because she was asked to come in so late in the evening. She was quick to direct the focus of Mrs. McLane's anger toward her, putting the blame on herself. "I was the one who asked Liam to fetch you." It had actually been Brett, but as far as she was concerned, that was a mere technicality. She was the one who had wanted the man's wife there.

A number of emotions washed over the pie-shaped face. "Why the hell would you do that?"

Alisha was precise in explaining her thinking. "Because your husband just had an appendicitis attack. I managed to take it out just as it ruptured." Her eyes never wavered from the woman's face. "I thought maybe you'd want to know that."

That her husband had just undergone surgery took some of the wind out of Henrietta's sails—at least for a moment. The woman looked at her uncertainly. "But he's going to be all right?"

Alisha was relieved to be able to give her a positive answer. "Yes."

"Oh." Rather than happiness, the news had indifference registering on Henrietta's wide, sun-lined face. "Tell him to get his butt home as soon as he can walk." And with that, the woman turned on her heel, pushed past Liam, retraced her steps to the front door and marched out of the clinic.

Alisha blew out the breath she hadn't even realized that she'd been holding.

"I'm beginning to understand why Nathan drinks," she commented to the man who had been serving Nathan for the past fourteen years. Anger underlined her words. How could anyone be so callous in regard to a person they were supposed to have loved? "I think if I was married to that impossible woman, I'd spend every evening drinking in order to forget."

Surprised that had just come out of her mouth, Alisha slanted a quick glance toward Brett to see if that had put him off. She was surprised—and maybe just the tiniest bit pleased—to see that her words had made him laugh.

"You're becoming one of us, Lady Doc," he told her, clearly amused by her declaration.

Several weeks ago, she wouldn't have been happy with that kind of a response. But hearing it now created a satisfied, happy feeling that caught her completely off guard. Feeling that way should have made her feel wary—but it didn't.

A FEW OF the regulars had remained at Murphy's, nursing their beers and waiting for news about their drinking buddy. The moment Alisha walked in, they all swarmed around her and Brett, firing overlapping questions.

"Is he gonna be all right?"

"He ain't dead, is he?"

"Did you have to cut into him?"

"Where is he? Did you send him home?"

"Can we go see him?"

Brett took over, raising his hand as well as his voice to quiet the men. "Lady Doc here took care of Nathan. She got him to the clinic just in time. If he'd stayed here with you bozos, he would have been dead."

Rather than question that, the men turned as if one to stare at Alisha. She wasn't sure what to make of it— and then one of the men said, "Let's hear it for Lady Doc!" The next second, a cheer went up. A couple of the men closest to her embraced her, exuding genuine gratitude. Stunned, she looked at Brett.

"Now you're really one of us," he told her with a broad grin, adding, "You did good."

The funny thing was, she really felt that way. For possibly the first time since she had decided to become a doctor, she felt as if her vocation and presence in a situation really mattered.

It was a while before she finally got upstairs to her tiny apartment. Two seconds after she closed the door behind her and opened her closet door, she was facedown on her bed, sound asleep.

THE KNOCK ON her door the following Sunday morning at eight didn't wake her. She had been up for a good hour. Expecting to spend a peaceful morning doing nothing whatsoever, the knock caught her by surprise.

This was supposed to be her day off, but obviously someone hadn't gotten the memo.

The old phrase about there being no rest for the weary ran through her head as she opened the door.

"You ready or do you need a few more minutes?" Brett asked.

He looked even more causal than usual, with faded jeans and a denim work shirt, both of which looked as if they had been through the wash a few too many times and adhered to his body as if they sensed they'd fall apart otherwise.

"You forgot, didn't you?" he guessed from the look on her face. With everything that had been going on these past couple of days, he could see how that had happened.

Rather than answer in the affirmative and admit that it had slipped her mind, she twisted her alibi into a question of her own. "You still want to take me to your ranch?"

"Why wouldn't I?" he asked her, then added, "Unless you don't want to go for some reason." He wasn't about to force her, but at the same time, Brett had to admit that he'd been looking forward to spending a little time with her without the demands of his job—or hers—getting in the way. "Up to you," he told her, leaning one broad shoulder against her doorjamb as he waited for her to think it over.

Instead of turning away or retreating into her apartment, Alisha remained there for a moment, thinking over the option he'd just given her. Since he'd kissed her that night at the clinic, she'd been a little afraid of what she'd felt, as well as somewhat leery of being alone with this man.

But at the same time, in the tradition of a moth moving around a flame, she knew she was more than a little drawn to Brett.

How about a lot drawn?

All the more reason not to be alone with him, 'Lish. You don't want to make the same mistake twice.

The problem with having a little voice that spouted common sense in your head, she'd discovered, was that the voice could easily be either ignored or overridden.

She did both.

"I'm ready," she told him, then glanced down at what she was wearing. Maybe not so ready, she decided. "I just need another minute or so. I'm not really sure what to wear," she confessed.

She looked fine to him just the way she was, he couldn't help thinking. "Any way you're comfortable is all you need to keep in mind," he told her, adding, "You're overthinking this. Forever isn't a formal kind of town. We don't notice outfits so much as we notice the person who's in them."

The way he was looking at her had her fighting a blush—and losing. To cover for herself, Alisha said, "Spoken like a true man. Women notice clothes."

"Well, since you're going to be the only female there, I don't think you have much to worry about." His eyes seemed to caress her as they passed over her again, as if inspecting what he'd just accepted. "You wouldn't have anything to worry about standing in a crowd of women and wearing a burlap sack."

Brett, Alisha couldn't help thinking, seemed to be able to say all the right things at just the right time.

Talk is cheap, remember?

She did remember. Remember that she'd gone this route before, with Pierce. She'd believed his stories, his lies and his initial protestations that he loved her.

This man wasn't Pierce. Pierce had only been in love with what he saw looking back at him in his mirror. He counted first, last and all the spaces in between. So far, she hadn't seen any evidence of that sort of egomania on Brett's part. On the contrary, he seemed to put everyone else first.

But then, Brett might have just been a better actor than Pierce had been.

Give the man a chance. He might surprise you.

"Something wrong?" Brett asked her. "You look like you're having some sort of a mental argument with yourself."

His intuitive assessment startled her—but she managed to recover nicely.

"No mental argument," she assured Brett—okay, she was lying, she admitted to herself, but under the circumstances, she could be forgiven the small white lie. She didn't want to let him in on her vacillation— or the fact that she felt as attracted to him as she did.

Right, like he can't guess.

With effort, she blocked the voice that seemed bent on tripping her up. "I'm just doing a quick mental check to make sure I'm not forgetting something."

Brett decided that she needed a little encouragement. The woman really needed to unwind a little. That was something that Dan had had to learn as well once he'd committed to Forever, he recalled.

"Nathan's recuperating at his friend's house, and the clinic's closed," Brett pointed out. For now, Nathan and his wife were taking a time-out, and Nathan needed his rest. "Looks to me like you're pretty free."

She didn't want to seem too eager. "There are things I have to consider that you don't know about," she told him primly.

He inclined his head. "Fair enough. What's the verdict?" Brett asked, instinctively sensing that if he pushed in any way, she'd push back, dig in and stay home. If nothing else, working at Murphy's had taught him how to read people and act accordingly. Alisha needed to come around on her own.

"That you're right," she answered him after a beat. "I'm free to leave."

There was a stillness in her voice that instantly alerted him. Were those nerves he detected? Was she nervous about spending time alone with him? Was the very thing he was looking forward to frightening her for some reason?

He'd begun to think of her as fearless, especially after he'd witnessed the confrontation between Alisha and Nathan's wife. Maybe at bottom, when it came to personal matters, she wasn't quite so fearless after all.

He did want her to enjoy herself as much as he just wanted to enjoy having her with him today. But he wasn't going to enjoy himself if she was uneasy during the whole time.

"Would you feel better if I had one or both of my brothers come along?"

The offer surprised her. That she was afraid of the feelings she might have for him was one thing. The fact that he *thought* there was fear involved on her part was quite another.

Alisha squared her shoulders like a young prizefighter about to go into the ring. "Why would I want that?"

"So you could feel more at ease," Brett answered simply.

"At ease?" she echoed. "Are you saying you think I'm afraid of you?" she challenged, indignation gleaming in her eyes.

"I'm saying I want you to enjoy the day on the ranch," he told her amicably, avoiding answering the question directly, "and I'll do anything I need to in order to ensure that you do."

He could word it any way he wanted to, but she knew what he was actually saying, and she wanted to make it clear to him that he was wrong—even if he wasn't entirely.

"I am not afraid of you," she emphasized.

He nodded, seemingly accepting her at her word. "Good. Then let's go."

"Absolutely." With that, Alisha walked out of the tiny apartment first.

Brett followed her, waited until she locked her door and then resumed walking behind her as they went down the narrow stairs. He hung back just enough to be able to watch her descent and to enjoy the view of that descent. He especially savored the way her hips moved from side to side.

It was a great deal like watching poetry in motion, he realized, his eyes never straying from the view.

It made him rather sorry that the stairway wasn't twice as long.

Turning around at the base of the stairs, Alisha looked at him, noting the expression on his face. "Why are you smiling like that?"

His sense of self-preservation had him quickly man-ufacturing a neutral answer. "Just looking forward to spending the day with you, Lady Doc. Just looking for-ward to spending the day."

Alisha had a feeling there was more to it than that, but she decided that it might be wiser to keep that thought to herself.

Chapter Fourteen

"This is all yours?" Alisha finally asked, breaking the silence.

They had been driving for a while now, and Brett had gone through a parted, partially rotting gate about fifteen minutes ago. She wasn't much when it came to judging distances, but that had to have been at least several miles back.

Accustomed to living in an area comprised of tall buildings with glimmers of grass every so often—usually pushing their way through cracks in the sidewalk—even after five weeks out here, this was a whole new experience for her. Here there was nothing but grass—and the occasional tree—no matter which way she looked. And the sky, she had to admit, was incredible, so blue that it almost hurt to look at it.

"Technically, that's what the will said," Brett answered. The ranch house was coming into view in the distance. He drove toward it. "But I'm sharing it with my brothers."

Somehow, she would have expected nothing less of him. She had come to realize that family was very important to Brett. Alisha caught herself thinking that her father would have liked him. A lot.

Now, where had that come from? she wondered defensively.

"Very generous of you," she told him.

He shrugged off the compliment—if that was the way she had meant it. With Alisha, because of the tone she used so often, he was never quite sure if she was being serious or sarcastic.

"Well, if it's one-third each theirs," he told her, "they'll be more willing to pitch in and help out when I need them."

Because she'd been raised to always strive for goals, to never just sit back and let things be, she assumed he had some sort of a plan for this ranch he'd inherited.

"So what are you going to do with it?" she asked.

He laughed shortly. What he intended to do with all this was still a mystery to him.

"Haven't a clue," he admitted. "Raise cattle on it or maybe horses. Or I could farm it—the soil's pretty rich."

"Are you considering selling it?" she asked.

"Why?" he asked with a grin. "Are you considering buying it?"

She was startled by the question, and it took her a second to answer coherently. "Oh, no, I'm not."

She didn't want to mislead him; it was just that if she'd inherited property like this, the first thing she would have thought of was selling it. But then, she hadn't grown up in these wide-open spaces. Maybe being a landowner appealed to him more than running that saloon of his.

"Right now, this is all just a big question mark to me," he told her, gesturing at the view before them. "About the only thing I do know is that the ranch house on it needs a lot of work."

He glanced at her to see if she was going to make a comment. The glance turned into a gaze. Her profile was even more striking in the morning light than it was inside his saloon with only the artificial light to enhance her features.

Damn, but she was beautiful, he caught himself thinking.

"Aren't you supposed to be looking at the road?" Alisha asked, pointing to the windshield and what lay beyond it.

"I checked the road," he drawled. "Don't worry. It's not going anywhere."

With the road wide open in front of him, there was very little danger of his running into anything as long as he checked periodically that there were no stray animals making a mad dash toward his truck's grillwork.

Alisha could almost feel his eyes studying her. Her adrenaline rose a notch, sending the blood rushing through her veins.

Had she made a mistake, agreeing to come out here like this with him?

"What's the matter?" she asked a little too casually, trying to cover up the fact that having him look at her like that made all sorts of things inside her grow skittish. "Didn't I get all the soap off my face this morning?"

"Your face is perfect," he told her softly. "Just like the rest of you."

Wow, she thought; if she'd been younger and more impressionable, that would have had her dazzled and floating at least five inches off the ground. But no more.

"I'm from New York, Murphy," she told him as crisply as possible. "Nobody sold me a bridge all the years that I lived there."

He knew what she was saying, that she thought he was just flattering her in an attempt to seduce her. It was more complicated than that, although the thought of seducing her was exceedingly appealing.

"Not trying to sell you a bridge, Lady Doc," he told her mildly. "Just telling it like it is."

She did what she could to steel herself off from his golden tongue.

"Where are you taking me, really?" she asked, doing her best to mask the butterflies that were wildly flapping their wings in her stomach.

"To see the ranch house," he answered simply, even though he knew she'd figured that part out for herself. "I thought I'd get your opinion."

She looked at him, confused. He'd mentioned that when he'd first asked her. Was he actually serious? *Her* opinion?

"Hate to break this to you, Murphy, but I know nothing about ranch houses."

"You can still tell if something looks like it's worth saving." It wasn't a question; it was a matter-of-fact statement. "But that's not the only reason I asked you to come out with me."

"Oh?" Here it came, she thought, bracing herself, wondering if this was where a really nice guy suddenly turned into a demanding male.

Brett nodded. "I just wanted to spend a little time alone with you before word started to spread."

What was he talking about? For a second, her mind was blank. Was he referring to the fact that he'd kissed her, and she had willingly kissed back? Did that somehow set her apart? She sincerely doubted it, not in this day and age, not even in a small town like Forever.

Alisha stared at him, not knowing what to make of what he had just said.

"By now," he went on to explain for her benefit, "everyone in town undoubtedly thinks you're a hero—or heroine, if you prefer."

For some reason, his words brought a sense of relief to her. "Why would they think that?"

"Well, you did save Nathan's life," Brett pointed out.

That part was true, but she was a doctor. It was what she was *supposed* to do, what she was trained for. There were no special accolades for that.

"I just did what any other doctor would do. My job," she emphasized.

The fact that she wasn't trying to make what she did come off heroic acted in her favor. He liked her modesty. Hell, he was realizing that he liked everything about her.

"The point is, we don't have any other doctor. Dan's hurt, so he couldn't have operated, and if you weren't here, we would have had to get Nathan over to Pine Ridge pronto. Pine Ridge is roughly fifty miles away. In the condition Nathan was in, the trip there with all its bumps and what have yous would have probably caused that appendix of his to explode on him. The upshot of it is that he would have most likely been dead by the time he arrived at the hospital. So, pure and simple, that makes you the heroine of the tale," he concluded, slowing down his truck.

"No," Alisha contradicted him, "that makes you a very imaginative man. It was no big deal." Although, she had to admit, if only to herself, that she was very satisfied—as well as gratified—with her own performance. Until that night, she had either assisted in the more difficult surgeries or performed a handful of very simple, by-the-book surgeries. Nathan's surgery had been way more complicated and taxing. Performing that appendectomy by herself, even under Dan's watchful eye, made it official. She was a real doctor now, she thought with pride.

"It is to Nathan," Brett was saying. He finally came to a stop, having pulled up in front of a weather-beaten, single-story ranch house that was badly in need of some tender loving care—and *soon*. "We're here," he announced needlessly.

Alisha managed to maintain a straight face as she asked, "How can you tell?"

"A sense of humor," he noted with approval. "Good. You're gonna need one if you decide to stay on in Forever."

Did he think she was still debating that? She'd just assumed that everyone thought she was staying on. The thought had made her feel somewhat trapped when she let it—as well as feel guilty if she decided to take off. The truth of it was, Brett's approach left her more inclined to consider staying in Forever. It wasn't freedom she required as much as the option of freedom.

She caught herself smiling.

"I'll let you in on a little secret," she told Brett as she unbuckled her seat belt. "I'll need a sense of humor no matter where I am." Getting out of the passenger side, she took a closer look at the outside of the ranch house. The paint was curling off in sections. "You weren't kidding, were you?" she marveled. Stepping clear of his truck, she surveyed the house slowly. The view didn't improve. If anything, it grew worse.

Brett shut his door and came around to her side. "About?"

She gestured toward the unhappy building. "The house needing work."

The structure was desperately in need of not just a fresh coat of paint, but it also appeared to be badly in need of structural repair. The sun had baked parts of the exterior, causing it to deteriorate to the point that there were sections that looked as if all she had to do was blow on them, and they would just disintegrate right before her eyes.

"Actually," she decided, "if the inside is as bad as the outside, I think you might be better off starting from scratch."

He'd already toyed with that idea, but he pretended that this was the first time he'd faced that option. "You mean just knocking it all down and building something brand-new?"

She nodded. Hands on her hips, she scrutinized the entire exterior.

"That would be my take on it. But maybe I'm wrong," she allowed, turning toward him. "Maybe the interior is fabulous, making it worthwhile saving the building."

The interior was just as bad as the exterior, but he refrained from saying as much for now. She'd see that for herself soon enough. Instead, he gamely said, "Only one way to find out."

Brett extended his hand to her.

After the briefest of hesitations, Alisha placed her hand in his. She pretended not to notice the flash of electricity that went through her—just as it had the last time. You'd think she would have gotten used to this, she silently lectured.

"Okay," she said, matching his tone, "Let's find out."

There were four steps leading up to the front porch

and the front door. Those, too, were in need of repair. Even more so, it turned out, than some of the rest of the house.

Her shoe went right through the rotting board. With nothing under her foot to support it, her right leg went straight down through the hole that had opened up when she put her weight on the step. Her body thrown off balance, Alisha started to fall.

She had no idea just how far down she might have fallen—the basement was right under the porch—had Brett not been holding her hand. The second the wood cracked and gave way, he instinctively pulled her back, keeping her above the ground. The sudden movement made her stumble backward against him, causing Brett to lose his footing. They both wound up falling backward to the ground.

Through sheer luck, Brett managed to break her fall by giving her something to cushion her body—him.

Flushed, the air momentarily knocked out of her, Alisha found it took her a second to orient herself and another full second to realize that she was lying right on top of him, face-to-face.

Belatedly, she realized that, thanks to him, she wasn't hurt.

The thought that he had taken the impact for both of them quickly followed. Horrified that Brett had gotten hurt because of her, she scrambled to one side while simultaneously apologizing and expressing her concern.

"Oh, my God, Brett, I'm sorry. Are you all right?" she cried, quickly scanning him for any bones that might have been sticking out awkwardly. None were. But that still didn't mean that he hadn't broken anything, she thought.

"I think my chances of running a marathon just diminished," he cracked.

She drew back to look at his expression. "Does that mean you're all right or delirious?" she questioned.

His mouth curved just the slightest bit. "Is there a third choice?"

She continued to scrutinize him as she hovered over him. The fact that Brett wasn't cavalierly getting to his feet worried her. She'd come to know him in the past few weeks, and this wasn't like him.

"You *are* hurt," she cried in dismay. He was hurt, and it was all her fault.

"Not sure yet," he answered honestly. "Taking inventory now."

Really worried at this point, Alisha went into doctor mode. She began pressing first one limb, then the other, working her way along each length slowly, gently and methodically.

When she saw him wince, she asked, "Does this hurt?"

"No." Brett's answer came out in a huff of breath as he exhaled heavily.

She didn't like the sound of that. Was he one of those macho males who refused to admit that he was suffering any pain until it turned out to be too late? Determined to be thorough, she kept on going.

"How about this?" she asked as her fingers kneaded the muscles along his other leg a little harder than before.

When he gave her a negative reply—which still didn't sound all that convincing to her—Alisha slowly examined both his arms. Somehow, she wound up being bracketed by them without fully knowing how that had happened.

It reminded her too much of an embrace that was about to happen. She deliberately moved a little back from him, even as she went on with the examination.

"Stop looking at me like I'm a sandwich, and you're hungry," she instructed, then chided when he didn't seem to be paying attention, "And you're not responding to me."

His smile was sly and managed to get to her at what seemed like the speed of light. "Oh, I'm responding to you, all right," he told her in a low whisper. "Maybe you should stop squeezing like that," he suggested. "You might get more of a response than you bargained for."

She could feel the blush taking over, turning her skin an embarrassing shade of pink. *Stop it. You're a doctor first, a woman second. Act like it!*

"Then you're really not hurt?" she questioned uncertainly. She was eyeing him with more concern than nervousness at this point.

One side of his mouth rose in a devilish half smile that she did her very best to ignore. "At least not where you can see."

On her feet first, Alisha extended her hand to him and waited.

Although Brett could get up on his own power—and did—he took hold of her hand anyway. Once on his feet, he continued holding her hand, his eyes on hers.

The silence grew deafening as it surrounded them. Having her land on top of him like that when his guard was temporarily down had caused havoc to run riot through his entire body, momentarily reducing him to a mass of needs and desires.

Reminding him just how very attracted he was to this woman, not just because of her looks, which he found stunning, but because of the person he had discovered beneath those polished looks. A person worth knowing.

"I'm a doctor," she heard herself saying to him, the words leaving her lips in near-to-slow motion. "Maybe we should step inside the house, and you can show me where it actually hurts."

Brett looked at her for a long moment, wondering if she knew what she was saying. He decided that she did—and not because it was wishful thinking on his part.

With a nod of his head, he released her hand. "Walk behind me so you don't run the risk of falling through another step. I wouldn't want to lose you."

Was that a flippant remark—or something more? *Wishful thinking, idiot,* she upbraided herself. *Get a grip!*

Alisha did as he instructed without comment, listening instead to the sound of her own heart slipping into double time.

She was acutely aware of the fact that she hadn't been with anyone since she'd thrown her engagement ring at Pierce.

Before, actually, since she and Pierce had hit a dry spell before the incident. The dry spell had gone on for almost a month because her schedule didn't mesh with his at the hospital. Each time she was free, he wasn't and vice versa.

It was only after she caught him making love to another woman that she realized their schedules hadn't meshed because Pierce had seen to it that they didn't. He'd told a mutual friend that he wanted to experiment with other women before *having to go through the charade of being faithful to a wife.*

She dwelled on the thought as a last-ditch effort to talk herself out of what she was about to do. After all, she'd sworn off having anything to do with good-looking men because of the disappointment they represented.

But thinking of Pierce didn't make her back away from Brett. Instead, it seemed to have exactly the opposite effect.

It made her feel things, need things, that all centered around this saloon owner/would-be cowboy with the wicked, wicked mouth.

They made it to the porch without further incident. The front door, she discovered, was unlocked. It was apparently in keeping with most of Forever, where people locked their doors only at night—if then. The other, more obvious reason the door was unlocked became apparent on closer scrutiny. Someone had taken the lock out, leaving a hole where metal should have been.

Alisha barely noticed. The beating of her heart, not to mention the fact that her whole being was heating to an almost dangerous degree, had her focused on only one thing: the man who was with her.

The man, she turned around to look at, who was closing the more-than-useless door behind him. The sound of it meeting the door frame echoed inside her chest, signaling a beginning.

"So," she began, her mouth inexplicably dry enough to safely house dust, "do you want to show me where it hurts?"

Brett slipped his hands into her hair, framing her face as he brought his mouth closer to hers. Yes, he ached physically, but that had more to do with her than the fall he had taken.

"Later," he replied. "I'll show you later."

"And now?" she managed to ask, her voice dropping down to a whisper as everything inside her scrambled for a vantage point, silently begging him not to turn away, not to bring her up to this throbbing expectation and then back off.

She'd had so many disappointments, she didn't think she could endure another one, even though this man wasn't the forever kind. He was just someone who had the power to dull the fierce ache, to silence the loud pain now echoing through her entire being. The pain that was bringing her to the edge of her resolve and having her teeter there, turning her into a casualty at any moment.

"And now," he whispered back, his breath feathering along her lips, "we have something else to do, something else to occupy us."

Drawing her in closer to him, he kissed her. At first very lightly, his lips hardly touching hers. All that did was cause the hunger inside both of them to escalate to an almost uncontrollable size.

He kissed her again, longer this time.

The third kiss absorbed them both and sealed their fate—even if neither one of them realized it at that exact moment.

Chapter Fifteen

Looking back later, it was as if a frenzy had seized her. Alisha felt a desire so large, so strong, she wasn't certain just how to approach it, how to begin to contain it, and she was far less certain just how she could appease it.

All she knew was that this desire consumed her, and she instinctively sensed that she would know no peace until she was somehow brought to that final, incredible pinnacle where all these demanding sensations were finally released.

That she was even thinking like this surprised her.

This just wasn't like her.

While, for the most part, she had enjoyed lovemaking with Pierce, the act itself had never been the foremost entity in her life. It certainly was never this all-pervading hunger that threatened to undo her if she didn't feel that exquisite sensation exploding throughout her body.

But this, this urgency, was quite unique. She'd sensed it the moment the lyrical dance between them had begun.

Everywhere Brett touched her, he made her crazy, fueling her need rather than satisfying her desire. Every pass of his lips along her skin, every caress of his warm, gentle hands just heightened her excitement, increased her need. Made her passions grow that much more volatile.

This was different. *She* was different because she felt if she couldn't ascend the summit with Brett, couldn't attain that wondrous fulfillment that each touch of his promised, she would disintegrate into a pile of ashes.

Eagerly, she tugged against his clothing, needing to feel his skin against hers, needing to touch him the way he was touching her.

She knew, *knew* this was insanity, yet she couldn't stop herself, couldn't just regain possession of her sensible side and back away. She *needed* to become one with him, even if it was for only a moment.

This had never been, even remotely, part of her plan for coming to this tiny dot of a place. She hadn't come here looking for love or even acceptance. If anything, the opposite had been true. She came here not to feel anything at all, to purge herself of the ability to *feel* anything at all.

But the exact opposite had happened. She knew that love was far too much to hope for, but some reasonable facsimile would do in its place. At least for now.

Brett made her feel gloriously alive. Somehow, when she hadn't been paying attention, he had managed to open the tomb that she had locked herself into. Opened it and brought her out so that she could see the sunlight. More than that, Brett had somehow succeeded in making her *want* to see the sunlight.

Single-handedly, he had brought light into her darkened world.

Her head was spinning, and she knew that half the thoughts running through her brain could easily be discounted as just so much rambling nonsense once they were dragged out into the light of day. But right now, at this moment, it was all making complete sense to her.

She let the last little tether that was anchoring her to reality go—and became completely his.

ALISHA WAS UNDOING HIM.

Layer by layer, she was stripping him bare, making him want her with an intensity that not only surprised him but downright unnerved him, as well. It did everything but rattle his teeth.

Lord knew he had never wanted for female companionship. Since practically in the cradle, he had been blessed with an easy charm that drew women to him like tiny iron filings to a giant magnet.

As far back as he could remember, he was never alone if he didn't want to be. But the attraction he held for the female of the species neither fed his ego nor gave him an inflated sense of self. It did, however, allow him to perceive the world in a certain light. He'd never once experienced wanting someone and being in doubt as to the outcome.

Here, despite the fact that Alisha was with him, in his arms, igniting him like a torch dipped in kerosene, he wasn't certain of her, wasn't assured that the next time he desired her this way, she would be here.

This match was different for him, and it both frightened him and intrigued him—mainly because what he was feeling gave this woman power over him, and he had never been in that sort of a situation before. He had *always* been the one with the power, the one in charge, and while he had never abused that power, never inflicted himself on a woman or had taken advantage of a situation, even in the most cursory of ways, he didn't know what it felt like not to be the dominant one.

Now he knew.

And yet, rather than run for cover, the way common sense would have dictated that he do, Brett wanted to be exactly where he was. Right here, in this moment, with this woman.

With each article of clothing he peeled away from her, he grew more inflamed, more eager to possess her. More hungry for the feel of her.

He didn't recognize himself.

It didn't matter. All that mattered at this moment was Alisha.

The furniture within the ranch house was large and comfortable and dusty. It was scarcely noticed and, for the most part, ignored. They moved from piece to piece, exploring one another, raising the stakes even as they raised one another's temperatures to dangerous new heights.

Did she realize how crazy she was making him?

Did she begin to understand what all this was doing to him? He doubted it. It was hard for even him to make sense of it.

The feel of her lips, skimming along his skin like the soft, fluttering wings of a butterfly delicately, fleetingly, perching on a flower, had his heart racing at speeds he hadn't thought possible.

He wasn't sure what turned him on more: when she teased him this way or when she allowed the full measure of her intensity to break through.

All he knew was that if he didn't have her soon, didn't completely lose himself within her, he would self-destruct.

Pulling her against him, he possessively stroked the length of her body, bringing both of them to the very brink of an explosive climax, then drawing back. He did it twice—until he wasn't able to hold himself in check a single microsecond longer.

Pushing Alisha back against the overstuffed deep green cushions of the sofa, he raised himself over her.

She was all that existed for him.

Bracketing her face with his hands, his eyes holding hers, Brett began to ease himself into her.

But what had started as an exercise in restraint quickly took on a life of its own. Shifting gears, he began to move his hips more and more swiftly against hers.

Hardly able to catch her breath, Alisha wrapped her legs around his torso, matching his every thrust, going ever faster and mimicking his every movement.

And then she was gasping for air as the euphoria seized her, bringing her up higher still until she finally felt Brett's arms tightening possessively around her. He moaned against her lips as they rushed up together to the very top of the peak. One lone, precarious moment and then they were suddenly free-falling down the steep incline together, clutching each other in an effort to preserve the moment.

To preserve themselves.

WHEN SANITY REAPPEARED, making its way to her on tiptoes, Alisha felt her heart pounding so hard, she was certain that it was going to leap out of her chest and then explode.

Gradually, she became aware of the fact that the weight of Brett's body was pinning her down to the cushions. Not hard enough so that she couldn't move if she wanted to, but just enough to allow her to feel every single ridge, every single muscle of his body as it lay pressed against hers.

The *thought* of his hard, nude body pressed against hers pinned her down more than the actual weight of it did.

With a blazing-hot haze still very firmly wrapped around her, Alisha thought she heard his voice. But for the life of her, she really wasn't sure if she was actually hearing Brett speak to her, or if she was just imagining the whole thing.

She strained to make out the words, if there actually were any.

There were.

He was asking, "Did I hurt you?"

Even now, in such a primal situation, he was being thoughtful. The thought made her heart swell.

She couldn't answer him right away. To do that, she would have had to have been able to breathe, and right now, that was an entirely tricky proposition.

It took her two attempts before she could finally manage one word. "No," and that came out in barely a whisper.

"I'm glad," Brett said, feeling her breath feathering along his chest when she answered him. Felt, too, his immediate response to her. His stomach was tightening into a hard knot even as desire was galvanizing the rest of him at an astounding rate. He wanted her again.

Another first, he thought, stroking her hair. That, too, was a first, he realized. He was actually content just to lie here with her head resting on his chest—somehow their positions had gotten reversed in the past few minutes—and her hair spread out all along his pectorals.

Definitely a picture that Rockwell would have painted

had the era the artist lived in been a bit more flexible, Brett mused as he continued to lightly run his fingertips along her hair.

Alisha raised her head to look at him, curious. "Why would you think you hurt me?" To her recollection, she hadn't done anything to indicate any sort of discomfort in any way. The exact opposite was true.

"I was afraid that I might have been a little too rough in my eagerness to make love with you," he told her honestly. He waited a fraction of a moment, then continued, thinking that if there was anyone he could be completely honest with, it was her—although *why* he felt that way, he really couldn't say. "I never wanted anyone with the intensity that I found myself wanting you," he admitted.

Now, there was a line if she'd ever heard one, Alisha couldn't help thinking.

But even as she raised herself up on her elbow to say as much to him—as well as let him know it wasn't necessary, that she really didn't expect this to lead to anything more meaningful than just perhaps another go-round of lovemaking somewhere down the line—the expression that she saw on his face caused her words to just fade from her tongue. The look in his eyes was so sincere, it stole her breath away.

Still, she forced herself to tell him, "You don't have to say that."

"I know," he told her, softly gliding his fingertips along her face. "I don't have to say anything." He lightly brushed his lips against hers. "But I want to. I want you to understand that I didn't have this in mind when I invited you to come see the ranch."

"You didn't?" she said, just the tiniest bit of mocking in her tone.

"Nope. If anything, I think I wanted to show off a little for you, maybe. Impress you with the cowboy side of me." The admission surprised even him, now that he said it. But he also realized that it was true. When was the last time he had wanted to impress *anyone?* He couldn't remember.

"The cowboy side of you?" she echoed.

Granted, she was aware that she was definitely in Texas, and there were cowboys around in this town, but she had never really applied that description to him. He was just Brett—and that was more than enough.

"Sure," he told her, slipping one arm around her and holding her closer to him. "No woman can resist a cowboy."

Turning toward him, she saw humor in his eyes. He was putting her on. Alisha played along. "Oh? And where's that written?"

He pretended to think for a moment. "I'm pretty sure it's in some rule book somewhere."

"I'm not impressed by cowboys," she told him matter-of-factly.

"Oh? Well, I'm fairly sure you're not impressed by the bartender in me."

Her mouth curved just a hint. "You're right. I'm not."

Brett sighed for effect. "You're a hard woman to impress."

"No, not really," she countered, growing serious for a moment. "I'm impressed by decency, by a man who cares for his friends, who cares for his brothers and doesn't put himself first all the time."

She put her hand on his chest and leaned her head

there for a moment as she studied him. If she didn't know any better, she would have said that she was falling in love with him, but she hadn't given herself permission to do that—not ever again.

But if she *was* to fall in love, it would be with him.

"You didn't tell me that you stayed in Forever to raise your orphaned brothers, even though you had a chance to leave town and follow your dreams."

He didn't like to talk about himself and deftly turned the topic sideways. "You're right. I didn't tell you. How did you find out?" he asked.

The smile she offered was damn near dazzling. He could feel its effects all through his body—a very potent reaction right now.

"You do realize that this is a small town, right?" Alisha asked.

He kept on looking at her, finding it hard to hold himself in check. He could feel himself wanting her as much, if not more, than he had just before they'd made love. Brett forced his mind back on the conversation they were having.

"Miss Joan." It wasn't a guess.

She moved her body into his, giving herself permission to savor this interlude a little longer. "That woman is better than a newspaper or a blog. I have *never* met anyone so full of information before."

"She's the town treasure, all right," he agreed. "Did you actually ask her about me?"

It wasn't a smile on her lips so much as a grin. "I didn't have to. Miss Joan was more than happy to volunteer all that information about you without a single question coming from me. She thought I should *know who I was up against*." Amusement highlighted all of her features as she continued. "Who I was renting a room from. I guess she really believes in that old Girl Scout adage, Be Prepared."

She was making him absolutely crazy again. Every breath she took, every word she uttered, had her body moving against his. Setting his on fire.

"I think that's actually a Boy Scout rule," he told her with effort.

"Whatever," Alisha replied with a careless shrug, a movement that managed to arouse him even more, if that was humanly possible.

Brett framed her face with his hands, lightly testing the waters before surrendering himself to the need that had risen up within him all over again with a fierceness and a fire that refused to be subdued.

"Remind me to send Miss Joan flowers," he murmured against her lips just before he deepened the kiss that swept them back into a world that only the two of them were allowed to inhabit.

"I TAKE IT you had a good day off," Holly said to her cheerfully when she walked into the clinic the next morning.

Alisha realized that she was humming and promptly stopped. Although she had a feeling it was a little late for that. Especially when she saw the expression on the nurse's face. As if Holly knew exactly what she was experiencing at this very moment—and what had caused this feeling.

"It was—interesting," Alisha admitted, deliberately choosing a word that seemed neutral to her.

"I think it was more than that," Holly told her with a knowing smile, then, for good measure, added, "You're glowing."

She was? Alisha couldn't remember being accused of that even when she had first become engaged to Pierce. Looking back, she realized that she hadn't felt this level of happiness, of contentment at that time.

Don't get carried away, 'Lish. This is just temporary, a wonderful, delicious interlude, not forever, remember?

"Must be the lighting," she said out loud with a shrug.

Holly laughed. "I don't think so. The lighting in the clinic isn't *that* good." They were alone in the clinic right now since the doors had just been opened and for once, there was no one waiting to get in. Even so, Holly still lowered her voice when she asked, "So, what did you think of Brett's ranch?"

Stunned, Alisha's mouth dropped open. Denial was the first thing that occurred to her. The second thing that occurred to her was that denial was undoubtedly probably futile.

So instead, she asked, "How did you know I went to see his ranch?"

"One of my brothers-in-law saw you and Brett driving to the old Robertson place. Rafe," she added for good measure, in case Alisha wondered who had spotted them.

Alisha sighed, shaking her head. "There is no privacy in this town, is there?" That still took some getting used to.

"Not so you'd notice," Holly replied matter-of-factly. "But on the plus side, there's always someone to turn to if there's a problem because we take care of our own and are there for each other the way people in the big city aren't."

Holly paused, as if debating whether or not to say

something. As a rule, she was rather quiet and tried not to interfere, but she'd blossomed a bit in the past year, after marrying Ray Rodriguez. "For what it's worth, I think that Brett is way overdue for some happiness of his own."

That was an odd thing to say, Alisha thought. If anyone in the town seemed to be carefree, it was Brett. Was she wrong?

"Oh? Brett Murphy didn't strike me as exactly being a solemn, unhappy man. His female customers seem to all flock to him." Even as she pointed that out, she realized that she was somewhat jealous of those women. Now, there was a new sensation for her.

Holly waved her hand at that. "That's just Brett's surface charm, but that's not who he is. He stepped up when first his parents died in a car accident and then when his uncle Patrick died suddenly. Took over running Murphy's and seeing to it that his brothers stayed in school, had the right work ethic, things like that. That takes a rare kind of man."

"Yes," Alisha quietly murmured. "I know."

Telling herself that she had to be careful and not fall into a trap that would ultimately spell disappointment was getting to be more and more difficult for her.

The door to the clinic opened just then, and she was relieved to see that their first patient of the day had arrived. It was time to get to work.

Chapter Sixteen

If she'd hoped that, despite Holly's inquiry, she could somehow keep the fact that she and Brett were seeing one another apart from the usual public encounters, that idea died a very quick death the first time she walked into the diner after being with Brett.

Miss Joan took one look at her, sidled up to her table with a fresh cup of coffee and happily observed, "Looks like someone had her candle lit."

She had made one vain attempt to discourage Miss Joan's assumption, feigning ignorance. "What does that even mean, Miss Joan?"

"Don't play dumb with me, Doc. You know exactly what that means. Neither one of us was born yesterday," Miss Joan had asserted with a decisive nod of her head before sauntering off with her coffeepot.

After that, Alisha saw no point in making any denials. She and Brett were together for however long *together* would last. Atypically, she made no plans for *tomorrow,* wanting only to enjoy today.

Her todays knit themselves together, and before she knew it, a couple of months had gone by. And then part of another.

It was all good.

EVER SO SLOWLY, Alisha eased the covers off her body and sat up, careful to do it very quietly. She took in a long breath and slowly exhaled it, focusing on nothing more than the moment.

It was hard to believe that over five months had gone by since she had arrived in Forever. The first few days she'd spent in the small town had felt as if they had moved with the speed of a three-footed, injured tortoise. The past month or so had raced by like the tortoise's nemesis, the hare.

That was because she was happy.

Right after she'd performed the appendectomy on Nathan McLane, everything changed. People's somewhat skeptical attitude toward her changed. They accepted her, and she'd found a place for herself, not only in the clinic, but in the general scheme of things in Forever.

Nobody brought up the subject of her possibly moving on anymore, not even Miss Joan. That part she knew was due to the fact that when she wasn't at the clinic, she was with Brett—or he was with her. The bottom line on that was that they were together.

Together. She liked the sound of that, she mused.

She was supposed to be getting dressed, but she lingered just a minute longer, focusing on her contentment. Alisha looked over her shoulder at the object of that contentment—the sleeping man in her bed.

Before she'd arrived in Forever, she would have bet everything she owned that she was never, *ever* going to even *look* at another handsome man, much less place herself in a compromising situation with one. And she certainly would never believe a single word out of that good-looking man's mouth. After all, she considered herself reasonably intelligent. At the very least, she wasn't a village idiot, doomed to be drawn to good-looking men, condemned to making the same mistakes over and over again in a vain hope that this time, the results would be different.

But then, it hadn't been Brett's extremely good looks that had won her over; it'd been his heart. He was a good, decent, kind man who just happened to have a face that could send a woman's heart racing at a hundred miles an hour.

At times, she had to stop, take a breath and allow herself to just be happy because there was still something inside her that was waiting for things to blow up, to go wrong. Waiting for paradise to fold up its tent and disappear into the night, leaving weeds and desolation in its wake.

But that had been her life before, with Pierce, not now. And she planned to enjoy the *hell* out of it until such time that it all ended on her.

Enough with this ruminating—she had hands to hold and medical wisdom to dispense.

Squaring her shoulders, she started to get up from the edge of the bed when she suddenly felt a strong, muscular arm snake itself around her waist, effectively immobilizing her.

"Don't go," Brett mumbled, part of his voice being absorbed by his pillow. "Not time to get up yet," he protested.

Not quite awake, he'd been watching her, or rather her back, and thinking to himself that he'd finally, *finally* lucked out, finally found a woman who he wanted to wake up next to for the rest of his days.

He'd given it time, patiently waiting for that feeling to fade. It only grew stronger with each day that went by.

The feeling was real. And so was she.

"Oh, more than time to get up, sleepyhead," she laughed, shifting on the bed to look at him more directly. "At least for me. You don't open that bar of yours for another few hours, so you can go on getting your beauty sleep. Me, I've got patients probably lining up even as we speak."

Brett didn't loosen his hold on her waist. "They'll wait," he assured her, his voice now devoid of its sleepy state. "It's not like there's another clinic they can take their business to. And Dan's there."

Alisha began to protest only to find herself being pulled back down on the bed. She thought of struggling, but that idea was without appeal.

"Dan's *not* there," she contradicted him. When Brett flashed her a look of confusion, she explained, "Now that his shoulder is better, he's finally getting ready to go on that vacation." That was one of the main reasons Dan had wanted an associate, someone to occasionally take over for him. "I'm supposed to be covering for him. That was the whole point of his getting a second doctor, remember?" Alisha pretended to peer into his face to see if any of this was ringing a bell. "Is any of this coming back to you?" she asked.

Brett shook his head, then said, "Maybe after I have my early-morning pick-me-up."

The gleam in his eyes caused her stomach to flutter. "Which is?" she asked in a hushed voice.

Raising his head for a second, he brushed his lips across hers before allowing his head to fall back against the pillow again. "Guess."

She really, really should start getting ready. Otherwise, she ran the risk of being late, and she prided herself on never being late. "Brett—"

The grin on his lips turned wicked. "You fight me on this, and it's just going to take you that much longer to get to the clinic. If you want my opinion," he said sagely, "you might as well surrender, Lady Doc."

"You'd like that, wouldn't you?" she said, still pretending to resist.

"You have no idea." He caught her earlobe between his teeth and sent a hot shiver down her spine before releasing it.

She could feel a thrill zigzagging all through her, taking her prisoner. Alisha laughed and surrendered. "Might as well," she agreed wholeheartedly, opening up her arms to him.

ALTHOUGH SHE HURRIEDLY threw on her clothes when it was over, Alisha was still late. She didn't get to the clinic until an hour later. The doors had been opened only ten minutes earlier, so she silently lectured herself that she hadn't committed a cardinal sin being ten minutes late. Cardinal sins clocked in at twenty minutes, a voice in her head that sounded oddly like Miss Joan said.

She supposed if she took that sort of a blasé approach, then she didn't feel too bad over having given in to herself—and to Brett. After all, it had been one exquisite, albeit far too short, detour to a haven that was exclusively theirs.

Without realizing it, she was humming as she crossed the threshold. Holly was already in the office, seated at her desk. Alisha was aware that there were several others in the waiting room when she breezed in, but if she stopped to see who, that would only make her that much more late. She could catch up with whoever was out there once she had him or her in her exam room. There was a great deal of merit in Dan's principle of getting to know the whole patient, not just a body part.

"Beautiful day, isn't it, Holly," she stated rather than asked the young woman. "I'll be ready in a couple of minutes," she promised as she crossed to the inner office door. "What's the schedule look like today?" she asked by way of conversation. "Filled to the brim?"

Holly raised her eyes to hers. Alisha caught herself thinking that she had never seen the nurse looking that withdrawn before.

"Not too full yet," Holly replied.

Alisha stopped walking and took a second look at the young woman. She didn't look ill, but she certainly looked uncomfortable. "Something wrong, Holly?"

"There're a lot of things wrong, starting with having to live in a town that could pass itself off as an inkblot."

The voice came from behind her. Alisha froze the second she heard it.

It can't be, her mind cried. It just couldn't be who she thought it was.

Please don't let it be him.

Because she refused to behave like a coward, Alisha squared her shoulders and her resolve as she forced herself to turn around.

Her heart sank.

A second later, her anger kicked in.

"What the hell are you doing here?" she demanded, her eyes narrowing into slits.

Pierce's smile reminded her of the Cheshire cat—it was cold and without an ounce of humanity to it.

"What's the matter, Alisha? Aren't you happy to see me?" he asked her.

Ever the egoist, she thought.

Wearing a freshly pressed three-piece dove-gray suit custom made for him by some trendy designer house, Pierce was far too dapper for his surroundings. She'd never seen anyone so out-of-place-looking in her life, and that included her during her first week here.

Since there were several other people in the waiting room, she didn't want to cause a scene. But neither did she want to sequester herself with him because that would somehow lead to allowing the man to believe he had the upper hand.

So she remained where she was as she bluntly answered his question. "No, I'm not happy to see you."

She saw anger flash across his brow before he said with deliberate, measured cadence, "Even though I've come to rescue you?"

"News flash—I don't need rescuing," she informed him tersely.

His laugh was dismissive, rude and condescending. "Oh, c'mon. You can't mean that. Living out here in this godforsaken place? Are you that far gone that you think you actually *belong* here?" he asked incredulously.

Out of the corner of her eye, she saw Holly picking up the phone and calling someone. The sheriff? she guessed. She wanted to handle this on her own, but it wasn't a bad idea to have a plan B if this turned ugly, she decided.

"The person who doesn't belong here is you," she informed him coldly. "Now, please leave."

Pierce shifted his weight, a sure sign of his growing impatience. "Can we go somewhere and talk privately?" It was more of a demand than a request.

A demand Alisha chose to ignore. "No," she said flatly. "Whatever you came to say, say it and then please leave."

Pierce glared at her, and for a moment, she was certain he was going to turn on his well-heeled shoe and storm out. But then, looking as if he was waging some sort of internal battle with himself, he said, "I came to tell you I was wrong. That I made a mistake and that I'm—I'm sorry." He all but spat out the last words, clearly not happy about having to say them in front of an audience of what he viewed as his inferiors. "If you give me another chance, I promise that I'll more than make it up to you."

She was well aware of the way he *made things up* when he was guilty of transgressions, and she didn't doubt for a moment that there would be more of them.

"I don't need more jewelry, Pierce." Her eyes locked with his. She was not about to back down. "And I certainly don't need more lies."

"I did a lot of soul-searching these last few months," Pierce began again, clearly seeking to wear her down and obviously fully convinced that he could.

She thought she was going to choke. "Soul-searching?" she echoed, stunned. "I wasn't aware that you had one."

His mouth turned ugly, but he caught himself at the last minute. "Okay, I deserve that. I deserve a lot worse," he conceded. "But I've changed, and all I want is a chance to prove it to you."

A pig had more of a chance of changing into a shining Boeing 797, Alisha thought, than he had of changing his ways.

"What's the matter, Pierce? Did you find out your grandmother put in a clause in her will that says you have to be married to someone your parents approve of before you can get the rest of your inheritance?"

She'd meant it as a flippant remark, but she saw something flicker in his eyes before they went completely flat. She stared at him in wonder.

"That's it, isn't it? For some reason, in order to get your hands on the rest of that money, you need a suitable match. Well, I'm sorry, Pierce, but breaking up with you was the second smartest thing I ever did."

"What's the first?" Nathan McLane, in for his post-op checkup, asked. The man, who had the place of honor as her favorite patient since he was responsible for everything else changing for her, leaned forward in his chair in order to hear her answer.

"Coming to Forever," she told Nathan.

"Shut up. This doesn't concern you," Pierce snapped at Nathan, his very stance threatening the man with physical harm if he said another word.

Nathan didn't only because someone else did.

"Wrong. Anything that concerns Alisha concerns not only him, but all of us," the deep male voice declared firmly.

Relieved and surprised, Alisha turned around to see that Brett had walked into the clinic. His very gait challenged the stranger in their midst.

Alisha still had to ask, "What are you doing here?"

He nodded toward the nurse, who finally relaxed now that he was here. "Holly thought you might need reinforcements."

"What she needs," Pierce informed him disdainfully, "is someone her own intellectual equal." His eyes swept over him contemptuously. "Not some dumb cowboy." Turning from Brett, he addressed Alisha. "Look, I messed up and I'm man enough to say it. Now, stop playing hard to get and let's get your things and get out of this two-bit rattrap. You don't belong here."

She took offense at his dismissal of the town. "Where I don't belong is with you," Alisha retorted icily.

Rather than curse at her and withdraw, Pierce grabbed her by the wrist and yanked her to him. "I said, stop playing hard to get, and let's go. You can make me *suffer* for my past sins when I get you home, if that makes you happy."

The next second, Pierce found himself being yanked up by the back of his suit jacket and spun around. "How about *I* make you suffer, instead?" Brett countered. "And Dr. Cordell's not hard to get. For you, buddy, the lady's impossible to get."

Rather than answer him, Pierce doubled up his fist, threw his entire weight behind it and took a swing at Brett.

Brett saw the punch coming a mile away and skillfully sidestepped it. For a split second, he debated his next move—was he going to be magnanimous or was he going to give this pompous ass what he deserved?

The next minute, he made up his mind and muttered, "Oh, the hell with it." He punched Pierce squarely on the jaw, sending the man sprawling down on the floor, howling in pain and cursing a blue streak. Brett grabbed him by his shirtfront and said, "Now, you listen to me and you listen well. If I ever find you coming back and bothering this woman again, if I hear that you're even *thinking* about bothering her again, there will be more things on your body that hurt than just your jaw. And I'm talking permanent pain. Are we clear on that?" he asked, shouting the question into his face.

Still holding his jaw, Pierce pulled away. He looked accusingly at Alisha. "You can't be serious. Him? You're picking *him* over me?" There was no way to measure how completely stunned he was over her choice.

"I'd pick him seven days a week over you," Alisha fired back. "Without even trying, he's ten times the man you will *ever* be. Now, get out of my clinic and out of my town," she ordered. "I have patients to see."

"You'll be sorry for this!" Pierce shouted at her.

"Only if I ever see your smug face again," she replied.

"You heard the lady," Brett said, taking hold of Pierce and *escorting* him out the door. "Leave!"

Brett remained standing there like a sentry, watching as Alisha's former fiancé got into his vehicle and drove away. He stood there for several minutes in case Pierce did a U-turn and came back in.

"He's gone," he told her.

His declaration was met with a smattering of applause that swelled and grew until everyone in the waiting room, as well as Holly, was on their feet, clapping with feeling.

Brett was concerned with only one person in that gathering. He crossed to Alisha, then held his hand up before her first patient of the day, Nathan, rose to follow her into the back of the clinic.

"Before she gets started, I'd like a minute to have a word with Lady Doc here," Brett said.

Nathan sank back down in his chair. "I've waited

this long. I can wait a little longer," he told Brett philosophically.

"Thanks." Brett nodded at him just before he secured Alisha's hand in his and hurried into the back of the clinic with her.

He went into the first exam room he came to and closed the door. While living in Forever was a lot like living in a fishbowl, this he wanted to keep between him and her until such time as he was ready for it to be made public.

"Did you mean what you said out there?" he asked Alisha.

"Probably," she allowed cautiously. "I said a lot of things out there. Which part are you asking about?"

She knew damn well what he was asking her. With a sigh, he spelled it out for her. "The part where you said you'd pick me over him."

He had to ask? she thought, surprised. "Of course I meant it. Pierce is a weasel and you're—not," she concluded, not wanting to flatter him too much and make him feel as if she was crowding him.

"And that's it?" he asked skeptically. "Nothing more?"

She hesitated, then asked, "Such as?"

It took effort for him to curb his impatience. "Such as you were his fiancée."

"Okay…" she replied slowly. She wasn't following him at all. "Brett, where's this going?"

How could he make it clearer than that? he wanted to know. "I'd like to have equal time. I'd like to have *more* than equal time," he emphasized.

The last thing she wanted to do was jump to the wrong conclusion and possibly ruin everything. So she shook her head and said—or began to say, "I don't—"

Okay, okay, he'd put his cards on the table. "I want you to be *my* fiancée— Oh, hell," he cried in frustration. "I want you to be my wife."

She blinked, feeling as though her head was short-circuiting, and she was hearing things. "Wait, you're going too fast," she protested.

"I can say it slower," he offered, then proceeded to do just that, saying the same words except repeating them in slow motion.

"No," she laughed, putting her hand over his mouth to stop him from going on. "I mean *this* is moving too fast. You haven't even said 'I love you'—"

He remedied that immediately. "I love you."

She shot him an impatient glare. "Like you mean it," she stipulated.

"Like I mean it," he parroted obligingly.

She had a distinct urge to punch him but refrained. "Damn it, Brett, this isn't funny."

Before she could say anything further, he caught her in his arms and held her to him. "No, it's not funny. It's very, very serious. Do you think I would have just asked you to be my wife if it wasn't?"

There went her nerves, frog-leaping over one another. "I don't know. Would you?"

"*No,* I wouldn't," he told her firmly. "And for the record, I've never asked another woman to marry me, and I suspect that I never will. So unless you want me to die alone, a shriveled-up old bachelor, you'll tell me you'll marry me."

She wanted to scream her assent, but she held herself in check. She wanted to make sure the man wasn't going to regret this in a few years. "And you're sure you really want to marry me?"

His grin was from ear to ear. "Never been surer of anything in my whole life."

She was quiet for a moment, taking stock of the situation. He held all the cards. And right now, she wouldn't have it any other way.

"I guess if I ever want to get out of this room and practice medicine again," she told him, "I'd better say yes."

It was done, settled, and he couldn't have been happier. She was his. "I guess so."

"Okay, then," she said obligingly, then paused before uttering a heartfelt "Yes."

Brett took her into his arms and said a split second before he kissed her, "Good answer."

And she knew that it was.

* * * * *

Don't miss Marie's next romance,
DIAMOND IN THE RUFF,
available October 2014
from Harlequin Special Edition!

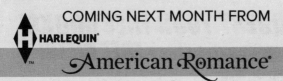
#1517 THE COWBOY SEAL
Operation: Family
by Laura Marie Altom

When Navy SEAL Cooper Hansen starts to have feelings for his brother's widow, Millie, he suddenly realizes this might be the most dangerous mission of his military career!

#1518 THE TEXAN'S SURPRISE SON
Texas Rodeo Barons
by Cathy McDavid

Jacob Baron wants to do the right thing for his newly discovered son. But the boy's aunt, Mariana Snow, has her doubts. Can he be the dad his boy needs—and maybe the man Mariana wants?

#1519 HIS FAVORITE COWGIRL
Glades County Cowboys
by Leigh Duncan

Hank Judd can handle his new job as ranch manager and might even survive the arrival of his ten-year-old daughter. Until the woman who broke his heart twelve years ago rides into town....

#1520 A RANCHER'S REDEMPTION
Prosperity, Montana
by Ann Roth

Dani Pettit and rancher Nick Kelly have been friends— *just* friends—for years. But after they share a scorching kiss, Dani can't forget it. Has she ruined their friendship...or discovered she's loved Nick all along?

REQUEST YOUR FREE BOOKS!
2 FREE NOVELS PLUS 2 FREE GIFTS!

HARLEQUIN®

American ★ Romance®

LOVE, HOME & HAPPINESS

YES! Please send me 2 FREE Harlequin® American Romance® novels and my 2 FREE gifts (gifts are worth about $10). After receiving them, if I don't wish to receive any more books, I can return the shipping statement marked "cancel." If I don't cancel, I will receive 4 brand-new novels every month and be billed just $4.74 per book in the U.S. or $5.24 per book in Canada. That's a savings of at least 14% off the cover price! It's quite a bargain! Shipping and handling is just 50¢ per book in the U.S. and 75¢ per book in Canada.* I understand that accepting the 2 free books and gifts places me under no obligation to buy anything. I can always return a shipment and cancel at any time. Even if I never buy another book, the two free books and gifts are mine to keep forever.

154/354 HDN F4YN

Name	(PLEASE PRINT)

Address	Apt. #

City	State/Prov.	Zip/Postal Code

Signature (if under 18, a parent or guardian must sign)

Mail to the Harlequin® Reader Service:
IN U.S.A.: P.O. Box 1867, Buffalo, NY 14240-1867
IN CANADA: P.O. Box 609, Fort Erie, Ontario L2A 5X3

Want to try two free books from another line?
Call 1-800-873-8635 or visit www.ReaderService.com.

* Terms and prices subject to change without notice. Prices do not include applicable taxes. Sales tax applicable in N.Y. Canadian residents will be charged applicable taxes. Offer not valid in Quebec. This offer is limited to one order per household. Not valid for current subscribers to Harlequin American Romance books. All orders subject to credit approval. Credit or debit balances in a customer's account(s) may be offset by any other outstanding balance owed by or to the customer. Please allow 4 to 6 weeks for delivery. Offer available while quantities last.

Your Privacy—The Harlequin® Reader Service is committed to protecting your privacy. Our Privacy Policy is available online at www.ReaderService.com or upon request from the Harlequin Reader Service.

We make a portion of our mailing list available to reputable third parties that offer products we believe may interest you. If you prefer that we not exchange your name with third parties, or if you wish to clarify or modify your communication preferences, please visit us at www.ReaderService.com/consumerchoice or write to us at Harlequin Reader Service Preference Service, P.O. Box 9062, Buffalo, NY 14269. Include your complete name and address.

HAR13R

Can't get enough of the **TEXAS RODEO BARONS**
miniseries? Read on for an excerpt from

THE TEXAN'S SURPRISE SON
by Cathy McDavid…

"Excuse me, Jacob Baron?"

Jacob turned. The woman looked vaguely familiar, though he couldn't recall where he'd seen her before.

"Yes."

She started toward him, managing to cover the uneven ground gracefully despite her absurdly high heels that had no business being at a rodeo. "May I speak to you a moment?" Her glance darted briefly to his brothers. "Privately."

"We were just heading home," he said.

"This is important."

After a moment's hesitation he said, "Go on, I'll catch up with you."

"No rush, bro," Jet said, a glimmer in his eyes.

"It seems you know my name." He gave her a careful smile once they were alone. "Mind telling me yours?"

"Mariana Snow."

Jacob felt as if he'd taken a blow from behind. "I'm sorry about your sister. I heard what happened."

Leah Snow. That explained why he'd found this woman familiar. Three years ago he'd dated her sister, though describing their one long weekend together as dating was a stretch. He hadn't seen her since.

Still, the rodeo world was a small one, and he'd learned of Leah's unexpected passing after a short and intense battle with breast cancer.

"Thank you for your condolences," Mariana said tightly. "It's been a difficult three months."

"I didn't know Leah had a sister. She never mentioned you."

"I'm not surprised." Mariana reached into her purse. "Leah didn't tell you a lot of things." She extracted a snapshot and handed it to Jacob.

He took the photo, his gaze drawn to the laughing face of a young boy. "I don't understand. Who is this?" He started to return the photo.

Mariana held up her hand. "Keep it."

"Why?"

"That's Cody Snow. Your son."

For a moment, Jacob sat immobile, his mind rebelling. He hadn't been careless. He'd asked, and Leah had sworn she was on birth control pills.

"You're mistaken. I don't have a son."

"Yes, you do. And with my sister gone, you're his one remaining parent."

The photo slipped from Jacob's fingers and landed on the table, the boy's laughing face staring up at him.

Look for
THE TEXAN'S SURPRISE SON
by Cathy McDavid,
part of the **TEXAS RODEO BARONS** *miniseries, in October 2014 wherever books and ebooks are sold!*